LE

There had been ... ... es were dripping with moisture. Kohler had left his luggage at the railway station and then had walked the short distance to his rendezvous in the Hofgarten. Herman was wearing a leather coat and a felt hat with the brim turned down all around. He looked, Kohler thought, like a Gestapo man left over from the days of the Third Reich. he also looked cold and displeased.

"You have to help me," Kohler said.

Herman shook his head. "Incorrect. I do not have to do anything for you."

"But I have carried out your orders."

"From your account of it, in a singularly clumsy manner, it would seem."

"The woman is dead. Does it matter how it was done?"

Herman made no answer, and they walked side by side for a few paces. Then Kohler said:

"You will help me to get back to the Democratic Republic? It is no longer safe for me here. When the body is found the police will be looking for me."

"That is so," Herman agreed. "Nevertheless, you will not be returning to the Democratic Republic."

"No?"

"No. We have other plans for you."

LETHAL ORDERS

JAMES PATTINSON

A Critic's Choice paperback
from Lorevan Publishing, Inc.
New York, New York

Reprinted by arrangement with Robert Hale Limited

ISBN: 0-931773-76-8

First Critic's Choice edition: 1986

Published in association with Interpub Communications, Inc.

From LOREVAN PUBLISHING, INC.

Critic's Choice Paperbacks
31 E. 28th St.
New York, New York 10016

Manufactured in the United States of America

CONTENTS

1

A FAVOUR

It was a dull day in Bonn, with the threat of rain hanging in the air like an impending punishment for things done or things left undone in the offices of government. It was the kind of day calculated to lower the spirits and induce a sense of depression even in the most effervescent of persons.

Gerda Vogel was not, even at the best of times, a person who could accurately be described as effervescent; she was of a stolid disposition, which seemed to be reflected in the somewhat dumpy figure and the lumpy contours of her face. Fraulein Vogel, nearing thirty, knew that she was never going to make the grade as a first-rate beauty, or even a second- or third-rate one for that matter; she had become resigned to the fact that she was an unattractive woman, that men did not turn their heads to take a second glance at her in the street, or try to make dates with her, or offer to buy her drinks in public bars; it had always been that way, and now it always would be.

Only Hans Kohler had ever acted differently towards her, had ever looked at her with desire, had ever treated her as someone to be picked out from the crowd of unmarried typists and secretaries who made up so large a proportion of the population of Bonn. Only Hans had ever made love to her.

On this dull grey day it was not the weather that was causing Fraulein Vogel's depression. Indeed, in the government office in which she worked in the tall glass-and-concrete building shaped like a giant shoe-box one was scarcely aware of the prevailing climatic conditions; one was insulated from them in a thoroughly artificial environment of central-heating, air-conditioning and electrical illumination. It was certainly not the weather, therefore, that was producing in Gerda Vogel such a feeling of acute melancholy, not the lowering skies or the threat of rain; indeed, it sprang from quite a different cause. She had a burden on her mind, and this burden was the knowledge that she had at last, after much stern mental struggle and not a few shed tears, decided to take a step which, once taken, would be irrevocable and which would almost certainly result in the break-up of her relationship with Hans.

It was three years since their first meeting, but she still had a vivid memory of that day, that splendid day when her whole life had been transformed. She had come to Bonn two years previously from her home town of Munster; they had been two dull, rather cheerless years, during which she had suffered much from boredom and loneliness. She had a small, comfortable flat where she spent much of her leisure time, reading, watching television, listening to gramophone records; but she knew that there was something missing, and she knew what that something was: there was no man in her life. And then Hans Kohler appeared.

She was eating a meal in a restaurant. It was rather crowded but she had a table to herself. It was a table for two, and he came up and asked a trifle diffidently whether she would object to his taking the vacant chair. She had an odd feeling that she had seen him somewhere before, but she could not remember where. He was slightly above average height and rather thin, with fair hair and bony features. She was not good at judging people's ages but she guessed that he was some years older than herself, possibly in his early thirties; not particularly handsome but not ugly either; no, certainly not ugly. She told him that she had no objection to his sharing the table; and she flushed and was annoyed with herself for doing so.

He thanked her and sat down; and then he introduced himself, though there was really no need for it.

"I am Hans Kohler."

She nodded, glancing at him nervously, shyly; meeting his eyes, pale blue eyes set a trifle deeply behind prominent cheekbones, and glancing quickly away again.

He waited expectantly for a few seconds; then: "And you?"

"I?"

"What is your name?"

"Oh," she said, and she felt herself flushing again, "I am Gerda Vogel." The flush faded, and she knew that her skin would be blotchy, because that was the way a flush always left it. Again she was annoyed with herself and was aware of the man's eyes regarding her. Self-consciously she wondered what he could be thinking of her. Was he noticing her gaucherie and being unpleasantly impressed by it? Perhaps. But why should she bother herself with what he might be thinking?

"Gerda," he said. "That is a beautiful name. My mother's name was Gerda."

"Was it?" she said, and could think of nothing else to add. In her embarrassment she took too large a mouthful of food and almost choked.

Kohler seemed to be perfectly at ease; she wished she had been able to match his self-assurance; how awkward he must think her. But he appeared not to be aware of any faults in her behaviour; he was not put off by her lack of response to his remarks; indeed, seemed to be doing his best to draw her out of herself. And if this were in fact his object, he was successful: she found herself relaxing, gradually replying at greater length, beginning under his subtle prompting to talk about herself, her work, her recreations, such as they were. He listened with apparently genuine interest, regarding her steadily with those pale blue eyes, the impact of which she found vaguely disconcerting. No one had ever shown such interest in her before, certainly no man, and she warmed to him more and more as the meal progressed.

She was sorry that it had to come to an end. Now he would leave her; she might never see him again. And she wanted to; there had never been anyone she so much wanted to see again; and again and again.

They left the restaurant together. She shivered suddenly in the cool night air outside, but it was not the coolness that had induced the shiver; it was the realisation that this was the moment of parting, when he would go his way and she hers.

"It's been so pleasant," he said. "I hope you were not bored with my company."

"No, of course not."

"Perhaps I talked too much."

"Not at all."

"Good-night then, Fraulein Vogel."

"Good-night, Herr Kohler."

With an effort of will she turned away and began to walk. With an even greater effort of will she resisted the urge to look back, to catch a last glimpse of him. People jostled her on the pavement, strangers going about their affairs, careless of any distress she might be feeling. She had a sense of loss, of having had some precious object in her hands and having allowed it to slip through her fingers. Why had she made no attempt to hold on to it? But what could she have done? She was nothing to Herr Kohler and it was ridiculous to suppose she was; he had merely been polite to someone with whom he had been forced to share a table; it would have been exactly the same if she had been anyone else. And yet she had an almost irresistible impulse to turn and run in pursuit of him before it was too late, before he vanished beyond recall.

She halted, a prey to indecision. Suppose she were to run after him; suppose she were to succeed in catching him; what could she say? That she could not bear to let him walk out of her life? That she needed him? That she had fallen instantly in love with him and could not live without him? She could imagine his reaction. He would think she was mad. How embarrassing it would be for both of them. And how useless.

She began to walk again. She had taken no more than half a dozen steps when she felt a touch on her arm. She glanced sideways and saw Hans Kohler beside her. She came to a halt, staring at him as though at an apparition.

"Forgive me, Fraulein Vogel," he said. "I see that I have startled you."

She struggled to regain her composure. "Yes, Herr Kohler, you did, a little."

"And now you are asking yourself why has this man followed me? You are thinking I presume too much on the strength of a chance meeting, a shared table in a restaurant. Is it not so?"

She shook her head. "No."

"No? Ah, you are being kind to me. Would you so much object if I were to walk with you a short way?"

"No, of course not. But I don't see —"

"There is no one you are going to meet?"

"No."

He seemed gratified to hear it. "Shall we go, then?"

They began to walk. Gerda Vogel could scarcely believe that it was happening, really happening, that it was not a dream, that he would not in a moment vanish again, leaving her treading the cold pavement, as she so often did, alone. She had wanted to run to him, but he had come to her as if in answer to a prayer. But why?

He seemed to read the unspoken question in her mind. "I am going to ask you a very great favour," he said.

"A favour, Herr Kohler?" She was surprised, even a little startled, by his words. She tried to think what kind of favour he could want from her, and her imagination was unequal to the task.

"I beg you to have pity on me."

"Pity?" She still failed to get the drift of what he was talking about. A frightening thought slipped into her mind: could he perhaps be slightly deranged? No; that was ridiculous; she had never met anyone who gave a greater impression of absolute mental balance.

"I am alone in this city; I live in one not very attractive room; I am sick of my own company. Would it be too much to ask if you would be generous enough to grant me a little more of yours?"

She wanted to assure him at once that nothing would make her happier, but somehow she could not find the words. He misinterpreted her lack of response and said quickly:

"But perhaps I am making a nuisance of myself. You have other things to do, more important things than being with me. I have no right to bother you. I will say again good-night, Fraulein Vogel, and this time I promise not to follow you."

He had come to a halt, and she halted too. He was turning away. She had to stop him, for if he went now it would be for ever.

"No," she said. "Don't go."

He turned again and faced her. "No?"

"No, Herr Kohler."

"Are you telling me that I am not to be dismissed for being so presumptuous?"

"It was not presumptuous," she said. "I shall be very happy to –"

He smiled. He had a very charming smile, little creases appearing at the corners of his eyes and mouth. Fraulein Vogel's heart was doing strange things. Kohler touched her hand and sent her pulse rate soaring.

"I also," he said, "am very happy."

*

There was nothing particularly hectic about the way they spent the evening. Kohler suggested a visit to the cinema and they watched a mediocre film. But for Gerda it was enchantment enough simply to be with him. They had supper at a small Italian restaurant which she had never visited before but which Kohler recommended. Afterwards he accompanied her back to the flat but refused an invitation to go in which she made with a certain hesitation.

"It has been," he said, "a most pleasant evening. I am grateful, Fraulein Vogel, for having been granted the privilege of your company."

There was an odd formality in his choice of words which chilled her heart. He made no attempt to embrace her at parting. She had been hoping for something; she did not know quite what, but certainly rather more than this, and she had a sense of anti-climax. She could guess what it was: he was weary of her already. What impulse had made him approach her in the first place she could not tell, but obviously he was now regretting it and wished only to break off the relationship before it went any further. She was disappointed but not surprised; it was no more than she might have expected; she had no physical attraction and he had found her a dull companion.

His parting words were a formality also. "I will keep in touch."

But of course he would not. She would never see him again. He had not given her his address, so if he did not come to her she would be unable to contact him. He had made sure of that.

Alone in her flat, she wept a little. It had been such a wonderful evening, opening up the vision of a future more delightful than anything she had ever experienced. She had been a fool of course to imagine that anything would come of it, to start building castles in the air which must inevitably tumble to the ground. Tomorrow morning she would be back at her desk; tomorrow evening she would be alone. The hours spent with Hans Kohler had been a brief, enchanting interlude, nothing more.

*

Three days passed; days of acute depression for Gerda Vogel. There had been no word from Kohler; he had vanished from her life as completely as though he had never existed. So did he perhaps not in fact exist? Had the whole evening's events been no more than a trick of her fevered imagination? There were moments when she almost came to believe that they had; for there was nothing tangible she could grasp as proof that there really was a Hans Kohler, a flesh-and-blood man who had taken her arm and begged her to grant him the favour of her company. Even his features were becoming less clear in her mind's eye, the outlines of his face blurring, so that she wondered whether she would even recognise him if she saw him in the street.

For three days she ate at the same restaurant where she had first encountered him, lingering at her table in the vain hope that he might walk in. Sometimes her heart would jump as she glimpsed a blond head in the crowd, but it was never his. By the third day she had become resigned: he was never coming back into her life.

And then, on the evening of that same third day, she heard the telephone ringing as she put the key in the door of her flat. She could not tell how long it had been ringing, and she almost dropped the key in her haste to get to the instrument. For she had a feeling that it was Hans and that if she did not reach the telephone before it stopped ringing he might never call again.

She left the door open and dropped her handbag and ran to the receiver and snatched it off its rest. She was breathing as rapidly as if she had sprinted all the way up from the ground floor instead of travelling effortlessly to the level of the fifth storey by means of the lift. All she could manage to gasp was the one word:

"Yes?"

"Fraulein Vogel?" It was a man's voice, but she could not be certain it was his; not entirely certain. Over the telephone voices could be so deceptive.

"Yes, this is Gerda Vogel speaking."

"Ah!" he said. "I am so glad. I was almost thinking you were not at home. This is Hans Kohler. Do you remember me?"

As if she could have forgotten! But why had he been silent those three interminable days? Did he realise just how cruelly he had tortured her? Had he done so purposely, vindictively? Was he some kind of sadist?

"I remember you," she said.

"And you are well?"

"Yes, Herr Kohler, I am well."

"Good, good. The weather is very pleasant, is it not?"

Oh God, she thought, does he have to ring me up merely to talk about the weather? She could have screamed into the mouthpiece, screamed in his ear. But she did not.

"Yes," she said, "it is excellent weather for the time of year."

She heard Kohler give a little cough. Then he said: "I am wondering whether you are free this evening."

She thought of telling him that she had an appointment. Why should she not tantalise him as he had tantalised her? But she dared not; it would have been too dangerous; she must do nothing that might possibly drive him away. And besides, she could not wait to see him again.

"Yes," she said, "I am free."

"And would it be too much to hope that you are not unwilling to give me the pleasure of your company for a second time?"

She did not answer immediately; she must not seem too eager. She counted slowly up to five, but she had scarcely reached that number when Hans Kohler was speaking again.

"But perhaps you have no wish to give up another of your evenings to me; perhaps you are thinking once is enough with that dull person. You do not need to be afraid to say so; I shall quite understand. Just say the word and I will go away and not bother you any more."

"No," Gerda said; rather hastily now, for it sounded as though he really meant what he had said; perhaps it would be all too easy to discourage him, and that was the last thing she wanted to do. "No, there is no need to do that. And I do not think you are at all a dull person."

"I am delighted to hear you say so. You have lifted my morale. Am I then to take it that you are not averse to spending another evening with a person who is not after all so very dull?"

She detected a note of laughter in his voice and could imagine the smile making those little wrinkles at the corners of his eyes. "If it will please you," she said, knowing that she was the one it would surely please the most.

"Excellent. So I will call for you in precisely half an hour, if that will be convenient."

"I will try to be ready."

He rang off then. She collected her handbag and closed the door. She felt untidy and grubby after the day's work, and she had only half an hour in which to make herself presentable. Just time for a shower and a change of clothing if she hurried. She had a feeling that he would be punctual to the minute and she did not wish to be half-way through her toilet when he arrived. In the event she was ready with five minutes to spare. She tried to be calm, but her pulse was racing and the sound of the buzzer caused a sudden acceleration in its rate. She took a deep breath and walked to the door.

She searched for any evidence of disillusionment in his eyes. Suppose he had been cherishing a picture of her in his mind that was altogether too flattering, and suppose the sight of her were to serve only to remind him of her woeful lack of physical charm. She had examined herself in the bedroom mirror, trying to convince herself that she was really not so plain, but without success: it was the same unattractive face staring back at her that she had grown so sick of with the passing years. But he seemed happy enough to see it; there was no apparent disillusionment; his smile was unforced, the smile of a man who was truly pleased to see her again.

"I would have called you earlier," he said, "but I was afraid."

She was amazed to hear him make such a confession. "Afraid, Herr Kohler! Of what?"

"Afraid that you might think I was forcing myself on you. That I might not be welcome."

She wondered whether he could really be telling the truth. She would not have credited him with so much diffidence. But perhaps he was not as self-confident as he appeared to be.

"So I waited three days; three tedious days. Then I could wait no longer; I had to speak to you again; I had to see you. Fraulein Vogel, do you realise that you have been in my mind ever since we parted three nights ago?"

"You are exaggerating," she said. But she wanted to believe that it was the truth, that he had been thinking of her just as she had been thinking of him.

Kohler protested with every appearance of sincerity that it was no exaggeration. She felt flattered. The voice of reason might warn her that no man could be so taken with her that he could not get her out of his mind, but she refused to listen to so cold a voice; it was far too pleasant to believe that Hans Kohler was the exception, the one man who could recognise the true intrinsic worth of Gerda Vogel. Beauty, it was said, was in the eye of the beholder; and so perhaps for him she was beautiful. At that moment she really felt as though she was.

It was a marvellous evening. She found Kohler even more charming, if that was possible, than he had been the first time. Soon they had broken down all formality and were calling each other Hans and Gerda. When they returned to the flat and she invited him in he did not refuse again. She made coffee and they sat together on the sofa, and after a while he began to make love to her. It was what she had dreamed about and desired above all things, but she was nervous nevertheless; she was fearful that he would be disappointed, would become disenchanted with her. She had to avoid doing anything wrong, anything that might repel him.

And then she heard his voice whispering in her ear: "I love you, Gerda. I love you so very much."

Could it be true? After so brief an acquaintance was it conceivable that he could really be in love with her? Yet why should it not be so? What did time have to do with it? Was she not in love with him?

She trembled a little when his hands began doing things no man had ever done to her before, but she did not move, made no resistance. She was nervous and excited and wildly, exhilaratingly happy.

"I love you," he said again. And she believed it, believed he was telling her no more than the truth.

*

It was hard to realise that that had all been three years ago; hard to realise how inexperienced, how gullible she had been then. She was more knowledgeable now, older, less likely to be misled by outward appearances. The Gerda Vogel of today would not so easily have been deceived by Hans Kohler's smooth approach. She knew now of course what his motive had been. Three years ago she had been only too willing to accept his protestations of love at their face value. Because she wanted him; she wanted him so badly that she simply had to believe.

And even if she had been able to guess at the hard purpose behind his love-making, would she have turned him away? Perhaps; but she doubted it. The need, the desire would have been too strong.

So was it not strong now? Yes, most certainly it was. She still loved him; nothing could alter that. But she could not go on with it; that was the crux of the matter. There came a time when you could go on no longer; a time when you had to call a halt because conscience had become too strong to be resisted further; a time when the voice inside had to be listened to and had to be obeyed.

For Gerda Vogel that time had come and the sacrifice had to be made, cost what it might.

2

A GIFT

Less than two months after their first meeting Hans Kohler moved into the flat with Gerda Vogel. She had never seen the room where he had been living, but she gathered that it was far from luxurious. He brought very little luggage with him: a suitcase and canvas bag contained everything. She wondered whether these represented the entire extent of his worldly possessions, but she did not ask him; though they were living together there was much about him that remained a mystery to her.

She had no idea what work he did. Whatever it was, it seemed to give him plenty of freedom; he was not tied down to any set hours and he was usually still in the flat when she left in the morning. She had given him a key, and he was able to come and go as he pleased. He appeared not to be short of money and insisted on paying his share of the living expenses. She would have been quite happy to support him from her own purse rather than not have him there, but she was pleased to accept his contribution: it showed that he was not professing affection for her merely for the sake of free board and lodgings. In spite of every evidence that he gave of sincerely loving her, she still could not rid herself of a niggling doubt, the feeling that this was all too good to be true, that it was a kind of dream from which sooner or later there would be a rude awakening.

And then one day he gave her a camera. The gift surprised her; she had never had any interest in photography and she had not imagined that Hans had either. And this was no ordinary camera of the kind that tourists and holiday-makers could be seen carrying around; although it was small, it looked expensive; he must have spent quite a deal of money on it. She was gratified but puzzled; the day was not a particular occasion, not as far as she could recollect an anniversary of any kind. So why this very expensive gift? She could see no reason for it.

Naturally she thanked him, but her pleasure was entirely for the fact that he should have thought of giving her something, not for the gift itself, which frankly she did not really want. She had no desire to take up photography; it had no appeal for her.

She looked at him in slight bewilderment. "But why give me this?"

"Don't you like it? It is an excellent camera," Kohler said.

"I am sure it is, and of course I like it. But I mean why give me anything? It's not my birthday, you know."

He smiled faintly. "Do I have to wait for your birthday to give you a present?"

So it was simply that he wished to give her something. How thoughtful of him. But why a camera of all possible things? Why not a small piece of jewellery or a wrist-watch, even a new handbag? It would surely have been more usual. But perhaps he preferred to do the unusual.

"Do you know how to use it?" he asked.

She shook her head. "You will have to teach me."

"Yes," he said, "I shall have to teach you. Because you must use it correctly, mustn't you? It would be useless otherwise, quite useless." He seemed to put a certain emphasis on the final word. She wondered why.

Later he gave a demonstration of how the camera should be handled. Oddly enough, the subject he chose was a page of a newspaper. He showed her how to get the print in focus, how to hold the camera and operate the shutter. There was nothing very complicated about the operation and she quickly got the hang of it.

"Good," Kohler said. "Next time we will put a film in it and see how skilful you are at making a photographic copy of the news."

She thought he must be joking but he appeared to be quite serious. "I don't understand," she said. "Why do you concentrate so much on this kind of thing? Surely there are far more interesting subjects to photograph."

Kohler disagreed. "No. This is what I wish you to do. It is for this kind of work that the camera is designed; it is for this sort of thing I have given it to you. When you have become proficient at taking pictures of a printed page you will be ready to take copies of documents."

She was startled. "Documents! What kind of documents?"

"The kind you handle in the course of your work. Government documents. What else?"

Again she thought he was joking; but there was still no smile on his face, and with a sick feeling in the pit of the stomach she realised that he was in deadly earnest. This was certainly no joking matter. She stared at him wide-eyed, the colour draining from her face.

"Oh, God!" she said. "Oh, my God!"

Kohler showed no emotion. "I think now that you begin to understand."

It was the truth; she was indeed beginning to understand, to understand only too well for her peace of mind. So many things were becoming clear to her now and putting an entirely new complexion on her relationship with Hans Kohler. That first meeting: had it really been as

fortuitous as she had imagined? Was it not far more likely
that it had been engineered by him? Perhaps he had been
watching her for some time, getting to know what kind of
work she did, everything about her. And then he had taken
the opportunity to make her acquaintance as if by chance
and had taken it on from there.

The strength seemed to go out of her legs and she sat
down suddenly on the velvet-cushioned sofa in that
comfortably furnished room of her flat which she had come
to love so much more since it had been shared with this
man. She felt crushed by the knowledge that he had merely
been using her; that his professed love for her was nothing
more than a sham; that in fact he had no more regard for
her than for a tool which he intended to use for his own
purpose. And that purpose? What could it be but spying?
She had heard of such things happening but had never
supposed that she herself could ever become involved in
anything of the kind. And that Hans – he of all people – the
man she loved – should be the one to play this sordid trick
on her. It was too much to bear. She began to weep silently,
the tears blurring her vision and dribbling down her cheeks.

"Come!" Kohler said sharply. "There is no need for
that. What is wrong with you?"

"You deceived me." She looked up at him accusingly.
"It's true, isn't it? All you ever wanted from me was this."

He did not bother to deny it, but merely answered:
"Why are you making so much fuss? What is there so
difficult in what I am asking you to do? It is a simple matter
after all."

"A simple matter to betray my country?"

He made a gesture of impatience. "Oh, let us not have
any of that nonsense. Betray your country by taking copies
of a few unimportant documents!"

"If they are unimportant, why do you want me to do it?"

"Because these things have to be done. It is a kind of international business. An exchange of material. Nobody thinks anything of it. It is accepted."

"You make it sound as though it were perfectly legal. But you know it is not."

Kohler shrugged. "What is legality? A convention. I do not accept the convention. To my mind what you will be doing is no more morally wrong than borrowing a book from a library."

Gerda Vogel dabbed at her eyes with a small square of handkerchief. She had stopped weeping and was recovering from the initial shock of revelation. But again she spoke accusingly: "You lied to me. You have never had any genuine feeling for me." This thing that he wanted her to do seemed to become of less importance than the fact of his deception.

He came and sat down beside her on the sofa. His voice became gentler, more persuasive. "That is not true." He took her hand and she allowed him to do so. "Oh, yes, I admit that my original reason for making your acquaintance was in order to make use of you. But how can you imagine after these months we have been living together that I have no feeling for you? How would that be possible?" He caressed her hand. "No, Gerda, it simply is not true."

She wanted to believe him, even while she suspected that he was lying. Suppose he had really come to love her, if only a little. Could any man so counterfeit a passion that was not at least to some extent genuine?

"Who are you?" she said.

He gave a laugh. "But you know who I am. Hans Kohler. Who else?"

She wondered whether even that were the truth. She had suddenly begun to have doubts concerning everything about him. And she knew so little; he had told her scarcely anything regarding his background and she had not pressed him to do so. Now, when she asked him who he was, she was speaking of more than the mere name, which meant nothing. But he chose not to understand the nature of the question.

He kissed her cheek. "I am your lover. Have you forgotten? I am the man who sleeps with you."

She did not respond to the lightness of his tone. "Who are your masters?" she asked.

But he did not tell her. "What does it matter? It is immaterial. It is better that you do not know such things. The less you know about me, the better it will be for both of us. Just accept me for what I appear to be."

Perhaps he was right; perhaps it was immaterial. Obviously the people he was working for were somewhere to the east, beyond the frontier, on the other side of that demarcation line that had been called the Iron Curtain.

"So you are a communist?"

"Oh, no labels, please," he protested. "Why bring politics into our relationship? You are a woman, not a political animal."

Again he was right; she had to admit that it was so. She had never bothered herself with conflicting ideologies.

"Come, now," Kohler said. "Is it not better to do this small thing I ask of you than to cast me out of your life for ever?"

She was aware of the threat in what he was saying. He was telling her that she had to make a choice: she must do what he had asked or lose her lover. She remembered the bleak emptiness of her life before he had come into it and knew that for her there really was no choice. She clutched at his arm, as though fearful that he might slip away from her, her fingers closing tightly on the sleeve of his jacket.

"I cannot let you go. I cannot."

He smiled faintly. "I knew you would be sensible, my dear."

*

Kohler was in fact an East German. He had been born in Leipzig soon after the end of World War Two and had grown up under the austere régime of the German Democratic Republic. In those days he had been Hans Schmidt and had acquired the name of Kohler, together with an excellent set of forged papers, only when he was ready to be smuggled into the Federal Republic in order to carry out the work for which he had been trained.

As a secret agent operating in West Germany an East German has very useful advantages: no one is going to guess from his speech or his appearance that he is not a native of the country in which he is working; the language is his own and he is familiar with the people and their customs. It is this which makes the task of counter-espionage such a difficult one for the Federal Republic to carry out effectively; agents from across the border are virtually indistinguishable from the men and women living farther to the west; they are indeed, whatever the markings on the map may indicate to the contrary, fellow Germans.

Kohler had been in West Germany for a considerable time before his steps were turned in the direction of Gerda Vogel. He had unobtrusively kept her under observation for several weeks before making contact with her in the restaurant; studying her habits, her movements; making sure above all that there was no man in her life. A fiancé or a lover would have made things difficult, and it was only when he felt reasonably certain that there was no such person that he decided to make his first move.

That Fraulein Vogel was not a physically attractive young woman did not bother him in the least; he was not looking for someone with whom he might become emotionally involved; on his side the affair was to be one of cool calculation, engaged in for one purpose only: the gathering of information to be passed on to his superiors.

Hans Kohler had no illusions regarding himself; he knew that he was not intellectually brilliant, and he had no desire to be. Nor was he ideologically motivated; he was a communist for no better reason than that he had been born in a communist state. Politics for their own sake did not interest him, and he was in the espionage business solely because it seemed an easier way of making a living than any other that presented itself to him. He was a conscientious, unimaginitive operator; the kind of reliable, painstaking man who constituted the backbone of a system which depended in its task of gathering information as much on quantity as quality. Kohler knew that in all probability nothing he might glean through the medium of Gerda Vogel would in itself be of earth-shaking importance, but he also knew that it was the patient gathering together of a vast amount of seemingly trivial items that was the basis on which the whole intelligence operation was built. With the help of Fraulein Vogel he hoped that he would soon be supplying enough documentary material to ensure his continued favour with those on whom he depended for his livelihood. His ambitions went no further than that.

He found the conquest of the woman less difficult than he had expected. Once the slight initial barrier of shyness had been broken down she welcomed him quite literally with open arms. From her appearance he would never have guessed at the eagerness with which she would respond to his love-making; there was a sheer animal sexuality about her that surprised him. Perhaps she even surprised herself in the abandon with which she yielded to him. He had foreseen a certain prudish resistance that would have to be overcome, but in the event she made it all so easy for him. He allowed a few weeks to elapse, the honeymoon period;

then, when he felt convinced that she would do anything rather than allow him to walk away from her, he presented her with the camera and told her what she had to do.

The reaction of shock, the tears, the accusations of deceit came as no surprise to him; they were no more than he had expected and they left him unmoved; he knew that in the end they would amount to nothing, that finally she would agree to provide him with the material he required.

*

She looked at him reproachfully, but she knew that for her there was only one way.

"No, Hans," she said, "I am not being sensible. I am being very foolish. But that is how it has to be."

3

CONSCIENCE

And now it had been going on for three years. For three years she had been taking copies of everything that passed through her hands at the Ministry. At first she had been fearful of detection; she had had visions of being arrested, brought up for trial, sent to prison; for months her nerves were frayed. But gradually she became hardened to it. It was all so easy. She was amazed at the laxness of the security system. It was not, of course, as though she were handling top secret material; the documents to which she had access were all fairly routine; but nevertheless she would have expected that rather more precaution would have been taken to ensure that they did not fall into the wrong hands.

Over the years Fraulein Vogel gained a reputation for conscientious devotion to duty. Everyone knew that if she had a job to finish she would continue to work on it after the other employees had left the office. And it was remarkable how often she did have a job to finish. Left to herself, she would take the camera from her handbag and get down to the real business for which she had remained behind. With practice she had become very skilful and it seldom took her more than a few minutes; it was almost as routine as her official employment and scarcely more exciting.

Kohler was pleased. His task was simple: all he had to do was to see that the films got into the right hands; and while the flow of material continued without interruption there seemed to be no reason why anything should change. For him it was a comfortable life; easy, undemanding and almost without risk. He was confident that he could rely on Gerda to play her part; she needed him and he had made it plain enough to her that she could have him only at the price of her continued devotion to the task he had allotted to her. In return he gave her the love she craved. It might not have been genuine love, but it was better than nothing; no one knew as well as she how much better it was than that. And at least she had a hold on him: as long as she supplied what he required she could be reasonably certain that he would not desert her. And how many women could be as sure of their men as that?

He congratulated her on the excellence of her work. "I can tell you that our people are very pleased with you."

It gave her no satisfaction to hear it, except in so far as the pleasure of those faceless men was reflected in Kohler's own attitude to her. If they were pleased he would be pleased also; that was all that mattered to her.

"Admit it now," he said. "You haven't found it such a difficult task to do, have you?"

She did admit that it was not too difficult now that she had got into the habit of it. Nevertheless, she still disliked what she was doing, and told him so.

"Why? Surely it is not your conscience that is continuing to trouble you?"

She thought about the question and was faintly surprised to realise that in fact she no longer had any qualms in that respect. It was amazing how quickly the sensibilities became blunted by custom. So why did she dislike what she was doing? Perhaps because she resented the necessity for it, the knowledge that only by such dubious means could she hold her lover, that she had to buy his attentions as a rich matron might buy those of a gigolo. Yet there must have been thousands of women who were content to do just that. One had to forget that the love was bought and paid for, to accept it as the genuine article and not demand the impossible. It was, after all, a most imperfect world, and how many people in it could truly be said to be happy?

And it could not be denied that Hans was keeping his side of the bargain; no man could have been more attentive, charming and considerate. As a lover he was all that might have been desired; so why not accept the situation and be content? It was the sensible thing to do, and Gerda Vogel was a sensible woman; she did accept the situation, and for nearly three years she was content and almost happy.

She herself would have found it difficult to say with complete certainty what caused the reawakening of her sleeping conscience. Possibly it was the result of a combination of causes, none of which would have been sufficient in itself to drive her to the step she had now decided to take. Certainly she had in recent months been taking an increasing interest in world news and had become concerned with reports of the growing might of Soviet Russia and her communist allies. In her mind there formed a picture of masses of tanks, guns, missiles and aircraft, along with vast hordes of armed men, waiting to cross the eastern frontier and overwhelm her country. Opposed to this monstrous threat was nothing but the frail screen of NATO forces, inferior both in numbers and equipment. If the men in the Kremlin should give the order for their armies to invade Western Europe what real hope was there of holding them back?

And she – what was she doing but giving aid to this implacable enemy. For purely selfish reasons she had allowed herself to be used as a pawn on the wrong side in this terrible game of international chess. She had told herself that what she was doing was of no real importance, that it could do no harm; but was that the truth? Who was she to judge the importance of her activities? How could she tell what use might be made of those documents which she was so assiduously photographing? If they had not been important why would Hans and the men behind him have gone to so much trouble to obtain them? Of course they were important, and of course she was bringing harm to her country by giving copies of them to the enemy. For three years she had been a traitor. It was an unpleasant word but it was the only one that fitted.

Well, she would be a traitor no longer; she would tell everything, make a full confession, even though it would mean losing Hans and facing a term of imprisonment. It was the only way she could make atonement for the crime she had committed. But she would not betray Hans; she could not bring herself to do that. She would tell him what she intended to do and give him time to get away. Perhaps he would slip back into East Germany. He would be lost to her but he would be safe.

*

He was not in the flat when she returned to it that evening. She waited in nervous impatience for him to come in, unable to sit still, moving restlessly from one to another of those pleasant, comfortable rooms which soon she must abandon for some far less attractive quarters. Almost an hour passed before she heard his key turn in the lock, and the sound of it sent a shiver down her spine.

When he came in he noticed immediately that she was in a highly nervous state.

"What is the matter?" he asked. "Something has upset you."

Instead of answering she fetched the camera he had given her nearly three years ago and handed it to him. He looked at it and then again at her.

"Is something wrong with it?"

"Nothing is wrong with it," she said. "But I shall not be using it again."

He laid the camera on a side-table, and came to her and put his hands on her arms. "Now what is all this about, Gerda? Why will you not be using it again?"

"Because I have finished with all that. I have decided to make a full confession."

He stared at her. "Have you taken leave of your senses?"

"No; I have come to them again. I realise now that I should never have allowed you to persuade me to do what I have been doing. It was utterly wrong."

"Isn't it a little late to come to that conclusion?"

"It is late certainly. But it is not too late. I cannot repair all the harm I have done but at least I can put a stop to it now."

"But this is insane," he said. "You know what they will do to you. Just because you confess, they won't let you go free. Or do you imagine they will pat you on the head for being a good little girl and tell you that your sins are forgiven?" There was a sneer in his tone. "Is that what you are hoping?"

"No; I know there is no possibility of that. But I am ready to accept my punishment."

"Then you are a fool." He was becoming angry and was shaking her. "A fool, a fool."

She broke away from his grasp and stood with her back to him. "I cannot help it. I have to do it. I am sorry, Hans."

"Sorry! Much good being sorry will do. And what about

me? Have you thought of that? Are you going to hand me over to the police? Is that part of your precious plan?"

She turned quickly to face him again. "Oh, no, no! How can you think I would do that? I would never tell them about you."

"How very kind of you," he said, sneering again. "You offer me the chance to run away, and for that I suppose I am expected to be grateful."

"I do not ask for gratitude." Her voice was very low, trembling a little. "I can see how it must seem like a betrayal to you. Believe me, it has not been an easy decision to make."

"Are you tired of me?" he asked. "Is that it?"

She made a quick denial. "Oh, no. You must not think that. I love you, Hans."

"A strange way of showing your love."

"I wish it did not have to be this way."

"But it does not have to be." His tone had altered; the sneer had gone and he was using persuasion now. He put an arm round her shoulders, drawing her to him. "Think what you will be giving up if you go through with this. There will be no man to sleep with you, make love to you, in your prison cell. Can you face that prospect?"

"I shall have to face it."

"There will be a long, lonely time to repent of a step taken too hastily now. And it will be no use thinking then of what you have thrown away simply to ease a pang of conscience. You will never get it back."

She was only too well aware of the truth in his words. He had unerringly found the weakest spot in the armour of her determination. Suppose she were to take this fateful, irrevocable step and then, later, to wish that she had not done so. She felt her resolve weakening in the face of Kohler's insidious arguments, in the warmth of his embrace. But she made an effort to resist.

"I can't go on doing the things I've been doing. I simply can't go on with it."

"Very well," Kohler said; and he sounded so reasonable and understanding that her heart warmed to him. "I appreciate your scruples. Perhaps I have put too much of a burden on you, expected too much. But there is no need to make a confession; that will help no one, for what is done is done. Surely, therefore, it will be enough if you simply stop collecting the material. There is no need to sacrifice liberty and happiness for some wild notion of expiation."

She felt the warmth in her heart increasing. He was showing her that there was an easy way out, revealing to her how she could have the best of both worlds. Was there, after all, any sense in making a martyr of herself, since that would not undo what had already been done? Surely it was enough that she should merely put an end to her treasonable activities. She felt an overwhelming sensation of relief, as though some black and threatening cloud had suddenly been blown away and the sun had come shining through.

"You would not mind?"

He gave a wry smile. "You cannot expect me to be very happy about it. I should, of course, prefer things to remain as they are, but if you really feel you cannot go on, so be it."

She would never have expected him to be so magnanimous. She was grateful to him for showing her how unnecessary was that fatal step she had so rashly decided to take. The relief was so exquisite that it made her weep. There remained one shred of cloud, however; one patch of darkness in a clear blue sky. She gazed at him, trying to read his mind.

"But you will leave me now?"

He did not immediately reply to the question. She waited anxiously for his answer, and it seemed to be a long time in coming, as though he had to give the matter a lot of consideration. Then he said:

"I don't think so. Not for the present at least. Why should I?"

"But if I am no longer supplying the –"

Kohler gave a laugh. "You think I am living with you only because of that?"

"Is there any other reason?"

"My dear Gerda, of course there is. I am happy living here. I like being with you."

His words astonished her. It was not what he had said in the past. But perhaps he had gradually come to have some regard for her, even to love her a little. Such things did happen. She tried to believe that it was so.

"And besides," he said, "you may change your mind. After a while you may decide that it was foolish to have any misgivings about what you have been doing. There will then be nothing to prevent you from starting again."

She answered quickly, vehemently: "No, I can never do that. You must not ask me to."

Kohler shrugged. "Well, we shall see."

*

He met the man he knew only as Herman in a rather seedy little café with steamed-up windows and a pervading odour of onion soup. The place seemed to be frequented mainly by working men in leather jackets and heavy boots. Across the road a building was in the process of being demolished, and the chatter of pneumatic drills could be heard. Kohler never met Herman in the same place twice, and quite often several months would pass during which they made no contact whatever. The films from the camera were deposited in a drop, a dead letter-box, to be picked up later. It was safer that way.

Herman drank some coffee, set the cup down and peered

at Kohler through gold-rimmed glasses, frowning slightly.

"She was going to make a full confession? To tell everything?"

"That is what she said. Fortunately, I was able to talk her out of it, to convince her that it was not necessary to go to such lengths."

"But why should she propose doing so at all?"

"It seems she has had an attack of conscience."

"Ah!" Herman said. "Conscience!" He made it sound like a particularly unpleasant disease. "Conscience!"

He was a plump-faced man with thinning brown hair and an unhealthy complexion. His suit, which was dark grey in colour, would have benefited from a visit to the cleaners; it fitted none too well and looked as though it had been slept in. Kohler had no idea where Herman lived or how he occupied himself when the two of them were not together; he knew nothing of Herman's private or public life, his tastes, hobbies or amusements, whether he was married or single, heterosexual, homosexual or bisexual; nor did he wish to know. He did not like Herman; he found the man physically repulsive and he was glad that their meetings were brief and of no greater frequency than was absolutely necessary for the business they had to transact.

"She seemed a trifle hysterical," Kohler said.

Herman shook his head. "That is bad. I do not like the sound of that at all."

"I am sure she will do nothing foolish."

Herman's voice hardened slightly, though he kept it low. The café was so noisy that no one but Kohler could have heard what he was saying. "How can you be sure? A woman like that ... it is impossible to be sure."

"She is in love with me. For my sake she —"

"We cannot rely on anything as unreliable as that. Is she going to continue with the work?"

"For the present, no."

"Then she is of no further use to us."

"She may start again later."

"Did she say so?"

"No, but —"

"Do you really think she will?"

Kohler had a feeling of being driven into a corner. "I don't know."

"But do you think so? Is it likely?"

"No," Kohler admitted with some reluctance, "I do not think it is likely."

Herman picked up his cup, drank some more coffee and set the cup down again with great deliberation. "She must be eliminated," he said.

Kohler had been expecting this, but he had cherished a faint hope that it would not come to it; that there would be some alternative.

"It isn't necessary."

"It is necessary. She is a risk, and we cannot afford risks. Some day she is going to have another attack of this ridiculous conscience and she is not going to tell you; she is going to make her confession without even asking for your advice."

"I don't think that will happen."

"I am not interested in what you think," Herman said coldly. "I am looking at possibilities, and the possibility is that Fraulein Vogel will give us trouble. I might even call it a probability. I see no reason at all why we should take such a risk when the remedy is so simple."

What Herman was talking about in his cold, passionless voice was of course murder. That he used another, less emotive word for it did not alter the fact. What he was saying was that someone would have to kill Gerda Vogel. And Kohler knew very well who he intended that someone to be.

Nevertheless, he asked: "Have you anyone in mind to carry out the job?"

Herman's pale eyebrows lifted slightly. "I did not think you would have needed to ask that question. What other person but you is so well fitted to perform this operation?"

"I would rather it was someone else," Kohler said.

"Why?"

"I have no taste for it."

Herman looked at him narrowly. "You have not become emotionally attached to this woman?"

"No, of course not. I am not a fool."

"Then why are you so squeamish?"

"I am not squeamish. I simply think it would be better if someone else did it."

"It would not be better. And it has to be you."

Kohler began to speak, but Herman silenced him with a gesture of the hand.

"That is an order," he said.

4

BOTCHED JOB

Kohler looked at Gerda Vogel, knowing what he had to do and not feeling happy about it. It might have been easier if he had felt an active dislike for the woman, but he did not. Though he had repudiated Herman's suggestion that he might be emotionally attached to her, and though this was probably true, it could not be denied that he did have a certain feeling for her, a feeling that, rather to his own surprise, had grown up in the years during which he had been living with her.

Certainly he did not love her; there was no question of that. He could have walked out of the flat never to return, and the break would have caused him no regret except perhaps for the loss of a comfortable, settled way of life. But he had no wish to harm her, to bring her existence to a sudden and violent conclusion.

And yet he had to do it. He had been given an order, a lethal order, and it was one he did not dare to disobey. Distasteful though he found the task assigned to him, he knew that the consequences of disobedience could be more distasteful still.

He had been waiting in the flat when Gerda returned from work, and she must have detected something unusual in his manner; a certain tension perhaps; for she said at once:

"What is wrong, Hans? Has anything happened?"

"Happened!" he said. "What do you suppose has happened?"

"I don't know. But you look – well – strange."

"In what way?"

"I can't describe it." She sounded hesitant. "But there was an expression in your eyes, in the way you looked at me when I came in. I felt a shiver go down my spine, as if I had seen a ghost."

"You think I am a ghost?" Kohler gave a laugh, though he was not feeling amused. Perhaps what she had seen in his eyes was death. "This is real flesh and blood, believe me." He stretched out his hand. "Touch it. Feel how warm it is."

She did not accept the invitation, and he let the hand fall to his side. He could see that his answer had done nothing to reassure her; she was receptive to his moods and had perhaps caught immediately some vibration, some vague warning even of what he intended to do. Or was that too fanciful an idea? Yes, surely it was; she would never suspect that anything so terrible could be in his mind.

And as if to confirm this conclusion she made no further remark on the subject but went into the kitchen and began to prepare a meal. After a few minutes he followed her and tried to get a conversation going, in order to smooth over the slight edginess that seemed to have come between them.

"Have you had a good day at the office?" he said, and was immediately struck by the utter banality of the question.

"It was much as usual," she said, without glancing at him. "Rather boring."

He was about to ask her whether she missed the excitement of the work she had previously done for him, but he decided not to. His eye was caught by a pointed cook's knife hanging from a hook on the wall, and the thought came into his mind that he had only to stretch out his arm and take it in his hand and plunge it into the woman's heart, and the job would be done. And he did in fact take the knife from the hook and hold it in his right hand while he tested the sharpness of the blade with the ball of his left thumb.

"What are you doing?" Gerda asked. There was no suggestion of uneasiness in the question. Kohler's ear was keenly attuned to the tone of her voice and he would have detected the slightest hint that she had read the dark purpose in his mind. "What are you doing with that knife?"

"I am thinking," he said.

"Do you need a knife to help you think?"

"It is about the knife that I am thinking."

"What about it?" She turned to face him now. She had been washing a salad at the sink and her hands were wet. She seemed puzzled, but still not uneasy.

She trusts me, Kohler thought. She trusts me utterly. It would never enter her head that I might intend to kill her.

"It is very sharp," he said.

"So?"

He made a pass with it in the air. "Has it ever occurred to you that this is a very deadly weapon, this innocent kitchen implement?"

"A kitchen is full of deadly weapons if you care to look. It is merely a question of using them for the wrong purpose."

"That is true," he said.

His gaze moved round the small, well-equipped room with all its modern labour-saving devices, its gleaming ceramic and chromium plate, and he could see a fine selection of tools which one might turn to the purpose of bringing a human life to an abrupt conclusion. But the knife in his hand was probably the best of them. He looked at Gerda, choosing the spot where he would need to thrust in the blade, the spot where there would be no bone to obstruct the steel, and the point would go slanting up to the heart. For it had to be done with one blow; that was the professional way: no frenzied multiple stabbing, but a single clear fierce thrust of surgical accuracy.

And then he lifted his gaze and met the woman's eyes, and knew that he could not do it like that; not with her facing him, watching him. It was just not possible.

"Something really is worrying you, isn't it, Hans?" she said. "I know it."

He denied it again. "I don't know what gives you that idea."

She was not convinced by the denial. "You've been somewhere today, haven't you? You've had a meeting with someone."

"And if I have?"

She looked worried. "Are they making trouble for you, Hans? Because of me?"

"No. No trouble."

But again she was not convinced. "That isn't true, is it? They are angry with you because of what I have done. You have told them."

"They had to know."

"And now they blame you?"

"No. Why should they?"

"But they're not pleased about it?"

"You could hardly expect them to like it."

"What are they going to do?"

"Nothing. There's nothing they can do. I think they hope that eventually I shall be able to persuade you to start again."

"I'm sorry, Hans," she said. "You know I can't do that. I have already told you. Never."

"Yes, I know. I accept it."

"I really am sorry."

She turned away and continued with what she had been

doing, not looking at him any longer. He still had the knife
in his hand. Now he could do it; now, when he did not have
to meet her eyes. His grip tightened on the handle of the
knife, but then he had a sudden mental picture of the blood
spurting from the wound, gushing out in a scarlet stream
over his hand, his arm, his chest. He hesitated; and then
she had moved away to the other side of the kitchen and the
moment had gone. He reached up and put the knife back on
the hook; doing it carefully, meticulously even, as though
he had been hanging a picture and had to have it exactly
right.

*

They talked very little as they ate the meal, facing each
other across the table. Kohler's mind was occupied with the
thought of what he had to do. He watched the woman
guardedly, considering the various methods open to him.
Poison would have been the easiest, but he had no poison.
Perhaps he should have asked Herman to supply him with
some; but Herman might have refused; probably would
have done so; would have said that it was not his
responsibility. It was so easy for him; he simply gave the
order and was not bothered regarding the method by which
it was carried out. Kohler felt a wave of resentment for
Herman, that plump man in the crumpled suit who gave the
impression of being utterly without human feeling.

"What are you thinking of?" Gerda asked suddenly.

"Nothing," Kohler said. "Nothing that would interest
you."

It was very far from the truth. What could interest her
more than the fact that he was thinking of ways of killing
her?

"You keep looking at me as if you were seeing me for the
first time."

She was wrong, he thought. He was looking at her as if

seeing her not for the first time but the last. But he did not tell her so; it might have upset her.

"Do you object to my looking at you?"

"No, but –"

"I like to look at you."

She said nothing more, and soon the meal ended and she got up and began clearing the table. Kohler did not offer to help; he had never taken any hand in the domestic chores and Gerda had never expected him to. While she washed the dishes he switched on the television and sat on the sofa, watching it without interest, scarcely aware of what was happening on the screen. When she had finished her work she came out of the kitchen and sat down beside him. He did not look at her.

Half an hour later he stood up, walked to a side-table and poured himself a glass of vodka. He drank it neat and put the empty glass back on the table. Gerda had turned her head to look at him as he helped himself to the drink, and then had once again given her attention to the television. He came up silently to the back of the sofa and stood behind her, his hands hanging at his sides. She did not turn, apparently engrossed in watching the picture in front of her. Kohler took a deep breath, lifted his hands and gripped her neck, his fingers pressing into her throat, choking her.

She began to struggle at once, clawing at his fingers and attempting to get up from the sofa. Kohler could feel her pointed nails scratching the backs of his hands and gouging the flesh. He ignored the pain, fighting to maintain his grip and dragging the woman's head towards him over the back of the sofa. He was beginning to sweat. Gerda was making half-stifled grunting sounds and her heels were thumping the deep pile of the carpet. He was surprised by the violence of her struggles to break free, and he was not at all sure that he could hold her long enough to choke her into insensibility. Too late he realised that he had been a fool not to employ some kind of ligature such as the cord of his dressing-gown or a nylon stocking; he had acted impulsively, unprofessionally, on the spur of the moment, without thinking the matter out. Now he was in trouble, because there was not enough strength in his hands to hold her much longer and she showed no sign of weakening in her struggle to get free. She was a well-built woman and no slender girl you could take in your hands and break as easily as a doll.

She made a final convulsive effort and broke away from him, falling forward on hands and knees between the sofa and the television set. From his position behind the sofa he was unable to reach her and he hesitated for a few moments, uncertain what to do next. Gerda was making a hoarse rasping sound as she fought to get her breath back, and he wondered whether to seize her from behind while she was still kneeling and make another attempt to strangle her with his bare hands. But he doubted whether a second try would be any more successful than the first, and he still had not made a move when she managed to get a hand on the television set and haul herself to her feet. She stood with one hand at her throat, staring at him across the sofa with horror and accusation in her eyes.

"You tried to kill me," she said in a low, trembling voice, as though scarcely able to believe the truth of what she was saying. "You tried to kill me."

Kohler made no answer; it would have been futile to deny the charge. He glanced down at his hands and could see the bloody gouges where her nails had scratched them. Certainly he had tried to kill her – and had failed. But he must try again; it had to be done; he could not leave it now.

"Why?" she whispered. "Why?"

He made a slight movement of the shoulders, as though repudiating any personal responsibility.

"Orders."

"Oh, my God!" she said.

He began to move round the end of the sofa. She retreated from him, backing away towards the door leading into the narrow entrance lobby. He followed her unhurriedly, and he could see that she was crouching a little, like a boxer taking up a defensive posture, her eyes watching him fearfully, as though he had been a wild beast threatening to spring. He wondered why she did not scream; perhaps it had not even occurred to her to do so. And then she spoke again, pleadingly, still in the same hoarse, low voice that was little more than a whisper.

"No, Hans, no! Please, Hans, please don't!"

He said nothing but continued to advance, slowly and inexorably. A moment later her back was against the door and she could retreat no farther. Kohler also came to a halt, again uncertain what to do. He stood quite still, looking at her and trying to think of a way of killing her – quickly, cleanly. She met his gaze for a moment; then with a sudden cry of terror, as though she had again glimpsed that picture of death in his eyes, she turned and began fumbling wildly at the handle of the door.

Kohler moved then. He dropped his hands on her shoulders and dragged her away from the door. Stepping back, however, he caught his heel in the carpet and fell over backwards, taking her with him, so that they sprawled together on the floor. He began hitting her, smashing his fist into her face, and he could hear the sound of a woman singing a mawkish love song on the television all the while he was hitting this other woman on the floor; this woman he had lived with, slept with, made love to, used, and now had no more use for.

She managed to roll away from him and get to her feet, and she ran stumblingly across the room towards the door of the bedroom, perhaps with the intention of taking refuge there and locking herself in. But Kohler was too quick for her; he snatched up the bottle of vodka from the side-table and holding it by the neck clubbed the woman with it on the back of the head. The bottle broke, spilling vodka and scattering fragments of glass on the carpet. Gerda's legs gave way and she fell sideways, collapsing on the floor.

Kohler stood over her with the broken bottle still in his hand. He could see that her eyes were open, and she was moaning faintly and making ineffective efforts to get up. He felt suddenly overwhelmingly angry with her for making things so difficult for him; she should have died more easily, but here she was, still moving, still struggling to remain alive in a perverse determination to thwart his purpose. He had never felt any hatred for her before but he did so now – a blind, unreasoning hatred. She was bleeding from the mouth; one eye was almost closed; her blouse was torn and her hair dishevelled. She looked repulsive and disgusting; a wretched object that had no right to be alive, yet was; alive and watching him with the one good eye and the one that was half-closed; watching him and afraid.

"Damn you!" he said. "Don't look at me like that! It was your own fault. You brought it on yourself with that damned conscience of yours."

He dropped the broken bottle and went into the kitchen and took the knife from its hook. It had come to that after all; she refused to die by other means, so it had to be that; it was all her fault.

He hoped she might be dead when he returned, but she was not. Somehow she had managed to get herself into a sitting position, her legs splayed out in front of her and her back supported by the wall. She was breathing noisily, as though she had difficulty in getting the air to her lungs, and when she saw him with the knife in his hand she lifted one of her own as if to ward off the expected blow, making a kind of whimpering sound like a frightened child.

Her obvious fear of him served only to infuriate him the more. Again he felt himself blaming her for everything that had happened; it was her perversity that had led to this situation and she had no right to look at him like that, to appeal to some feeling of pity in him that did not exist.

He bent down and struck at her suddenly. He felt the knife go in a little way and come up against some obstruction; and he knew that he had not done it professionally, had not missed the bone, had not thrust straight to the heart. He heard the woman give a scream; not loud but curiously high-pitched, like a thin, ghostly whining. He dragged the blade out of her flesh and struck again and again, frenziedly, the way he had told himself it must not be done. And the blood was coming now, coming in a warm flood, straining her blouse and her skirt, staining the knife and the hand that grasped it.

She was no longer making any sound. She had fallen over on to her side and her head was touching the floor. She was no longer looking at Kohler; she was not looking at anything. She was not even breathing.

Kohler dropped the knife beside the body and straightened up. The thing was done, but it had been done badly; there was no denying that. It had been a botched job, messy, amateurish, not at all as he had hoped it would be. Nevertheless, the fact remained that it was done; it was finished; he had carried out his orders.

He looked at his bloody hands and went into the kitchen and washed them at the sink. He had not been wearing a jacket but there was blood on his shirt. He stripped it off and found a clean one in the bedroom. He took a blanket off the bed and returned to the sitting-room and covered the woman's body. The television was still switched on and a comedian was telling a joke. Kohler was in no mood for jokes; he walked over to the set and switched it off.

The sudden silence in the flat was curiously eerie. Kohler

again looked at his hands and then at the blanket-covered heap by the wall. He was not sweating any more, and he felt cold, even though the room was warm. He tried to think what he must do next. He could not dispose of the body; that was quite out of the question. It would have to remain where it was until someone found it. And he must leave the flat, get away from there without delay; there was no time to waste; every minute that he stayed there increased the danger to himself.

Yet still he made no move. Once again he glanced at his hands, as though half expecting to see the blood clinging to them yet. But they were clean; he had scrubbed them thoroughly and there was not a trace of that incriminating stain remaining on them. Only the gouges scratched by the woman's fingernails still bore witness to the struggle that had taken place such a short while earlier, and they were no longer bleeding. He gave a sudden laugh, turned and walked into the bedroom. He put his suitcase on the bed and began to pack his belongings.

By the time he had finished packing he was beginning to think more coolly, and he came to the conclusion that it might after all be wiser not to leave the flat at once. He had to have somewhere to sleep and it was rather late to go looking for a hotel room at that time of night. Besides which, a hotel might not be the safest place for him in the circumstances. The best plan would probably be to stay where he was for the present, leave early in the morning and get in touch with Herman.

*

There had been some rain in the night and the trees were dripping with moisture. Kohler had left his luggage at the railway station and then had walked the short distance to his rendezvous in the Hofgarten. Herman was wearing a leather coat and a felt hat with the brim turned down all round. He looked, Kohler thought, like a Gestapo man left over from the days of the Third Reich. He also looked cold and displeased.

"You have to help me," Kohler said.

Herman shook his head. "Incorrect. I do not have to do anything for you."

"But I have carried out your orders."

"From your account of it, in a singularly clumsy manner, it would seem."

"The woman is dead. Does it matter how it was done?"

Herman made no answer, and they walked side by side for a few paces. Then Kohler said:

"You will help me to get back to the Democratic Republic? It is no longer safe for me here. When the body is found the police will be looking for me."

"That is so," Herman agreed. "Nevertheless, you will not be returning to the Democratic Republic."

"No?"

"No. We have other plans for you."

"Ah!" Kohler was not sure whether to take this as good news or not. It all depended of course on what those other plans were. Evidently they had worked out another assignment for him, and it was good to know that he was still a trusted agent, but it would be too much to hope that the new job would be as comfortable as the last. He had had three years of soft, easy living; perhaps now he was going to be made to earn his pay with rather more difficulty. He glanced at Herman's pale, heavy face. "But I shall be leaving Bonn?"

"Oh, undoubtedly. You will, however, be going somewhat farther than East Germany, and in quite a different direction."

Kohler waited for more precise information but was

disappointed. Herman took a slip of paper from his pocket and handed it to him.

"For the present you will go to this address. You will ask for a man named Steiner. You will stay there and await further instructions."

Kohler was about to speak but Herman stopped him. "No questions. You have your orders."

There was a path branching off to the right. Herman made a smart right turn and walked away. Kohler watched him for a moment or two, then looked at the paper in his hand. There was only one thing to do: he had better pick up his luggage and go to see the man named Steiner.

5

FALLACY

It was a cold, clear December day when Sam Grant of the
Peking Inquiry Agency found himself at the wheel of his
Cortina driving down into the Essex countryside. He was
on his way to interview a client who lived in a place called
Yew Tree House in a village named Bellingham All Saints.
Grant was not terribly enthusiastic regarding this errand,
since he very much doubted whether anything at all
interesting would come of it. However, Mr Peking had told
him to go down there, and as it was that gentleman who
paid his salary he had had no alternative but to go.

Yew Tree House turned out to be one of those weathered
old buildings that look as though they have lived through a
couple of centuries of occupation, if not more. Grant was
not well enough versed in the architectural line to put an
exact or even approximate date on it, but anyone could tell
at a glance that it was pretty ancient. The brickwork had
acquired the patina of age, and though the paint was in
good condition, it was of a dull brown colour which
produced a rather sombre effect. There was a porch over
the door with a bay window on each side of it, and the door
was of bare oak with some wrought-iron hardware which
had possibly been fashioned by the village blacksmith long
before anyone imagined that such fittings would become

highly fashionable after most of the blacksmiths had disappeared.

As far as Grant could see, there was no blacksmith in Bellingham All Saints now; the village consisted of little more than one meandering street, a church with a stone tower and a slated roof, a few houses scattered haphazardly around, a public-house called the King's Head and a small general store.

Grant had to drive the entire length of the village before coming to Yew Tree House. It stood well back from the road behind an untidy garden enclosed by a low flint wall, and the yew tree, which might have been as old as the house itself, was on the right of the gateway. Grant parked his car at the side of the road, walked up the weedy gravel path to the front door and rang the bell. A few moments later the door was opened by a prim-looking middle-aged woman who peered at him with an air of suspicion.

"Yes?"

"Miss Rogerson?"

The woman shook her head. "I am Miss Saunders – Miss Rogerson's companion. Would you be good enough to state your business, young man?"

The voice in which this formal request was uttered seemed to match the woman's appearance. Grant resisted an inclination to smile and gave his name.

"I'm from the Peking Inquiry Agency. I believe Miss Rogerson is expecting me."

Miss Saunders treated him to a further careful inspection, thin lips pressed firmly together and pale blue eyes probing for signs of deception perhaps; but finally she seemed to accept him for what he said he was and admitted that Miss Rogerson was indeed expecting him. She made this admission with a touch of distaste, as though to indicate that she personally did not approve of inquiry agents in general or this one in particular.

"You had better come inside, I suppose."

She made room for Grant to walk into a chilly entrance hall and closed the door. The hall had a tiled floor and there was a trailing fern in a pot on a high stand giving off a faintly earthy odour, as though a portion of the garden had inadvertantly wandered indoors and had not been able to find the way out.

"Wait here," Miss Saunders said in a tone of command; and she walked across to a door on the other side of the hall, opened it and disappeared from Grant's line of sight. Almost immediately she reappeared and said: "Come this way. Miss Rogerson will see you now."

Miss Rogerson was sitting in an armchair on one side of a cheerfully blazing log fire. Miss Saunders hovered in the doorway after ushering Grant in, perhaps hoping for an invitation to make a third party at the interview, but Miss Rogerson dismissed her with an imperious flutter of the hand and she went away, closing the door behind her.

"Do sit down, Mr Grant," Miss Rogerson said, indicating a chair on the opposite side of the fireplace. "I am glad you were able to come."

She was a large woman, who had probably been quite a beauty of the statuesque type in her younger days. She was rather letting herself go now; perhaps indulging too much in the wrong kinds of food and not taking enough exercise. Her hair was auburn and there was no evidence of grey in it. It might have been dyed, but Grant doubted it; she looked the sort of woman who would not give a damn about her appearance.

"How is Alexander?" she asked.

Grant had to think twice before realising that she was referring to his employer. Somehow Mr Peking never came into his mind in association with his Christian name.

"He is in excellent health," he said.

"We are old friends, you know; though it is some years

since we last met. Perhaps he told you."

"No," Grant said, "he didn't tell me." He wondered just
how close the friendship had been. The idea of a romantic
attachment between the black-bearded, mountainous Mr
Peking and the statuesque Miss Rogerson seemed wildly
fanciful, but perhaps when both had been a lot younger
there might have been something of the sort. And it could
explain why Peking had sent him so promptly down to this
Essex backwater in answer to Miss Rogerson's call for help.
The other explanation that had been in his mind – that the
woman was immensely rich – seemed less likely now; there
was nothing here to suggest any great wealth, though of
course appearances could be deceptive.

A dreamy look came into Miss Rogerson's eye. "Ah, yes.
Alexander and I –" She broke off and seemed to return
abruptly from some far-off time and place to the present.
"But any reminiscences of mine are hardly likely to be of
interest to you, Mr Grant."

Grant was not so sure about that – if the reminiscences
also concerned Mr Peking. It might have been very
interesting indeed to catch a glimpse of some part of the
great man's personal background, which had always been
shrouded in mystery. But he did not say so.

"You are wondering of course why I require the services
of a private detective," Miss Rogerson said. "Well, I will be
perfectly frank with you, it is not a matter on which I would
have called in a person of your profession in the normal
way. But suddenly I thought of Alexander and I felt sure he
would help. He is such a generous, warm-hearted man."

Grant had never regarded Peking as either generous or
warm-hearted, but perhaps there were occasions when he
could be. "What kind of help is it you need, Miss
Rogerson?" Peking had told him nothing regarding the
type of assignment it might be. Possibly he had not had any
details himself.

"It's my niece, Angela. Angela Harka." She spelt it out for him: 'H, A, R, K, A.''

"What about Miss Harka? It is 'miss'?"

"Yes. Her father was Czechoslovakian. He came here in the War. He and my sister are both dead. They were killed in a car accident when Angela was twelve years old. I am her only close relative, so naturally she came to live with me. I regard her more as a daughter than a niece."

Miss Rogerson paused.

"But she is not still living with you?" Grant said.

"Oh, no. It is rather more than three years since she left. Living here, I suppose, became too quiet and dull for her. She just had to go to London; nothing else would satisfy her."

"Is she still there?"

"I imagine so."

"You mean you don't know?"

"Well, no, not for certain. You see, I haven't heard from her for nearly a year."

"Oh," Grant said, "I see."

"The fact is, the last time she came down here we had a quarrel. She flew into a temper, said she never wanted to see me again and walked out of the house. Since then we have had no contact whatever."

"What was the quarrel about?"

"Oh, something very petty. I made some criticisms regarding her way of life and she resented them. You know how young people are. So touchy."

Grant wondered just how much of the touchiness had been on Miss Harka's part and how much on Miss Rogerson's. The thing must have been building up for some time to end in such a drastic break. Perhaps the aunt had been too interfering and the niece had finally had enough.

"How old is Miss Harka?" he asked.

"Twenty-two and a few months."

"And she has a job in London?"

"She's had several. She's restless. I don't know what she's doing now. Perhaps nothing. She has a private income, you see; not terribly large, but enough to live on. From her parents' estate."

"So what do you want me to do?"

"Well, to tell you the truth, I'm rather worried about her. I'm afraid she may have got into bad company."

"And you'd like me to see whether she has?"

"Precisely. You can tell me what kind of people she's consorting with and so forth. One hears so much these days of the sort of things that go on."

"Wouldn't it be better if you went to see her yourself, Miss Rogerson?"

"Oh, no; certainly not." She was very quick to reject the idea. "It is not for me to go to her."

Grant saw that there was a question of pride involved. He guessed that Miss Rogerson would have liked to be reconciled with her niece but could not bring herself to make the first move.

"You think she should come to you?"

"Naturally, if she wishes to heal the breach; it was she who caused it. Besides, I have not been to London for at least twenty years; I detest the place. Moreover, if I were to visit Angela she would almost certainly consider that I was poking my nose into her private affairs, and that would only make matters worse."

"You want me to poke my nose in, though?"

"But only discreetly. I am sure you know how to be discreet, Mr Grant. Alexander assured me that you were a most competent man."

"That was nice of him."

"And I am sure he was not misleading me. If I may say so, Mr Grant, you make an excellent impression. I feel that you are a person to be trusted."

Grant wondered whether Miss Rogerson was indulging in a little flattery. Perhaps. On the other hand, perhaps she meant what she said. Women of her generation tended to prefer the clean-shaven male with the neatly-trimmed hair and the slightly conservative style in clothes. And though he said it himself, at the age of thirty-five or thereabouts Samuel Grant was very far from running to seed. So, taking all in all, why should the lady not be favourably impressed? Why, indeed!

"I try to do my best," he said. The kind of job Miss Rogerson was handing out hardly promised to be an exciting one, but who wanted excitement all the time? Of course you could never be sure; an assignment that looked perfectly straightforward and simple might turn into something very different, as he knew from experience; but he could see no indication here of anything but a rather dull routine piece of work. Well, it was a way of earning your bread. "Can you give me Miss Harka's address?"

"I can give you the address she was at when last I heard from her, but of course she may have moved. If so, I suppose you'll have to do some detective work in order to trace her."

"I'll jump that hurdle when I come to it. She may not have moved."

"That is so." Miss Rogerson got up from her chair, walked to a bureau and made a search among some old letters. "Ah, here it is. I'll make a copy for you." She wrote out the address in block capitals on a sheet of notepaper and handed it to him. "It's a flat she was sharing with another girl named Carol Donson."

"Do you know Miss Donson?"

"No. I have never met her."

Grant glanced at the address, then folded the paper and slipped it into his pocket.

"I wonder whether you have a photograph of your niece

which you could let me have. So that I'll recognise her when
I see her."

"Why, yes." Miss Rogerson searched in the bureau
again and came back with a small colour snapshot. "It was
taken two or three years ago. She'll be older of course."

Grant examined the photograph and saw a slender girl
with straight blonde hair cascading over her shoulders. The
face was rounded, pleasant enough in appearance but with
no pretensions to classic beauty. Angela Harka looked the
kind of girl it might be fun to go around with. He put the
photograph in his wallet.

"You will have some tea before you go?" Miss Rogerson
said.

Grant politely refused the invitation. "I had better be
getting back to London."

                              *

He came in through Epping Forest, and when he reached
Woodford he decided to go straight to the address Miss
Rogerson had given him. It was in the Chelsea area and it
was not so much a flat as a basement. The front door was
about six feet below the level of the pavement and there
were some iron railings enclosing a flight of worn stone
steps leading down to it. The door was painted a pale green
and had a bell-push on the left.

Grant went down the steps and put his thumb on the
button and heard a muffled buzzing sound on the other side
of the door, but nobody came to open it. He tried again
with the same result, and came to the conclusion that there
was no one at home. He gave a shrug, walked back up the
steps and was making his way to the place where he had left
the Cortina when he saw a girl come round the corner some
twenty yards further on.

The girl was wearing zip-up leather boots, a camel-

coloured winter coat with a belt and a white knitted hat
with a bobble on the top. Grant paused by the Cortina and
waited for the girl to go past. He could hear the clicking of
her heels on the pavement, and he turned his head and saw
her reach the place he had just left. She went down the
steps and he followed her as far as the railings and got there
just as she was pushing a key into the green-painted door.
He could see that she was certainly not Miss Harka, so he
said:

"Excuse me, but are you by any chance Miss Donson?"

She turned away from the door and looked up at him.
There was a nearby street-lamp throwing enough light
down into the area where she was standing to reveal an oval
face with a kind of pixie look about it. The hair showing
below the knitted hat was dark brown and short, and she
had dark eyes and a mouth which seemed to go up at the
corners and a slightly pointed chin. She was not very tall
and she reminded Grant of a girl he had known a long time
ago and had been half in love with before they had drifted
apart.

"Yes," she said, "I am Miss Donson. Who are you?"

"I'm Sam Grant."

"Do I know you, Mr Grant?"

"No, you don't know me. As a matter of fact it's Miss
Harka I'm looking for. I believe she lives here."

"What do you want with Miss Harka?" the girl asked, a
shade warily, it seemed. She was still standing with the key
in her hand at the foot of the steps, while Grant stood at the
top.

He thought of making up some likely story but decided
that the truth might be more advisable. When you told a
story it all too often led to awkward complications later.

"I've just come from her aunt, Miss Rogerson. She asked
me to call in and see her."

"She's not here," Miss Donson said.

"I know. I rang the bell."

"Well, that seems to be that then, doesn't it?"

She was not being very helpful, Grant thought. And it had begun to rain.

"Look," he said, "don't you think we might go inside? It's getting rather wet out here."

"You're asking me to let a perfect stranger into my flat? That wouldn't be a very wise thing to do, would it? How do I know you're not a con man – or worse?"

"I give you my word I'm not."

"Well, you would, wouldn't you? It hardly rates as absolute proof."

Grant descended two steps, bringing himself a little closer to the girl. "Do I look like a con man?"

"I don't know. I've never seen one. Not that I can recall. And anyway, I expect they vary quite a lot." She paused and seemed to be giving him a pretty close inspection. Then she said: "Still, maybe I'll take a chance; you've got an honest face."

"Thank you."

"But if you should think of trying anything I ought to warn you that I'm an expert at judo."

"I'm a Black Belt myself," Grant said. It was a lie, but he doubted whether she had been telling the truth either.

She gave a laugh, and he could tell that she believed him no more than he believed her. She did not give the impression of being at all nervous, however, and he would have made a guess that she was not the kind of person who easily took fright.

She turned the key in the lock and pushed the door open. "Come along in then."

It was a lot better inside than might have been expected from looking at the exterior. It was pleasantly warm and nicely furnished. Miss Donson got rid of the coat and the woollen hat, and Grant was able to see her rather more clearly in the better light of the room into which she had conducted him. She reminded him less of that girl of days gone by, but he liked the look of her; he liked the look of her very much indeed.

"So," she said, "you want to see Angela. Why?"

"I told you. Her aunt asked me to call on her."

"Why?"

"It seemed a natural thing to do."

"The way I heard it, they're no longer on speaking terms."

"Well, yes, it seems there was a quarrel of some kind. But that doesn't prevent Miss Rogerson from being concerned about her niece."

Miss Donson treated him to a bit more probing with her fine dark eyes, which were set rather widely apart and had a faintly oriental look about them. "Are you really a friend of Miss Rogerson?" she asked.

Grant hesitated a moment and decided that it might be time for a little more of the honesty. "Frankly, no. The fact is, I'm a private inquiry agent employed by Miss Rogerson."

"To spy on Angela?"

"I wouldn't put it like that. She's rather worried about Miss Harka. All she wants to do is find out what kind of people she's associating with and so on."

"If that isn't spying, I don't know what is."

Grant was beginning to doubt whether honesty had been the best policy after all. He seemed to have roused some resentment in Miss Donson. He made an attempt to repair the situation.

"I know that's what it must sound like, but you should appreciate Miss Rogerson's point of view. She looked after Miss Harka from the age of twelve, and it's understandable that she should still have a close interest in her welfare. I'm quite sure there's no cause for concern, but you do see how it is. I've got to make a few inquiries before I can reassure Miss Rogerson. I thought you might be able to help me. Sharing a flat with Miss Harka, you must know just about everything there is to know about her."

He was still getting the impact of Miss Donson's lovely eyes, and he could detect very little warmth in them.

"You really have got a nerve, haven't you, Sam Grant?" she said. "I don't know whether to admire you or despise you. Why should I tell you a damn thing about Angela?"

He could see how the thing must look to her, and he knew that he had played it all wrong. He had assured Miss Rogerson that he would act with discretion, but he could hardly claim to have done so. He was obviously not going to get any information from Miss Donson, and it was a dead cert that she would tell Miss Harka about him. He must be losing his touch.

"No reason at all," he said. "Maybe I'd better be on my way."

"Maybe you had," she said.

But he made no move towards the door; he just stood where he was, gazing at Miss Donson and feeling no inclination to stop doing so.

And finally she said: "Oh, look, I'm simply dying for a cup of tea. Would you like one?"

"Well, thank you," he said. "That's a very generous offer to make to someone you find so despicable."

She gave a laugh at that. "Yes, it is, isn't it? But that's me all over – generous to a fault."

She went away to get the tea, leaving him to make himself comfortable in one of the armchairs and wonder whether Miss Harka was likely to walk in at any moment and find him there. He hoped she would not, because it might make things a trifle awkward. But she had still not put in an appearance when Miss Donson came back with the tea. When she had given him a cup she sat down and said:

"So you want me to tell you how Angela is behaving herself? You think she may be going around with the wrong set, smoking pot, sniffing coke, pumping heroin into her veins and generally living it up?"

"I don't think anything of the sort," Grant said. "You don't give me the impression of being in that kind of business yourself, and since she's sharing this flat with you it seems reasonable to suppose that she isn't either."

Miss Donson took a sip of tea; then said: "That's a brilliant deduction, but it happens to be based on a fallacy. She isn't."

"Isn't what?"

"Isn't sharing this flat with me."

"No? But I understood from Miss Rogerson that —"

"That she was? Yes, I know. And she used to, but she doesn't any more. Something came up and she moved out."

"Am I allowed to know what the something was?"

She drank some more tea before answering, and she seemed to be thinking it over. But finally she must have come to the conclusion that it would not be betraying a confidence.

"Well, I don't suppose it's any secret," she said. "It was a German named Kurt Muller. She's living with him now."

6

A CALL ON MISS HARKA

Mr Alexander Peking gazed at Grant across the large teak desk which separated them, frowning slightly.

"I don't like it," he said.

"Why not?" Grant asked.

"Living with a German. I don't like the sound of that at all."

"What's wrong with it? Why shouldn't she live with a German if she wants to? Germans are okay these days; we're not at war with them now, you know. All that Nazi business is past and done with. We're Common Market partners and NATO allies."

"I know, and I wish we weren't. Joining the EEC was the worst thing this country ever did. Those people over there," – Mr Peking made an airy gesture with one fat, pink, carefully manicured hand in the vague direction of the North Sea or the English Channel – "they're not our sort, you know."

"You mean they work harder than we do?"

"No, I do not mean that. I mean they're not to be trusted. Never were."

"Oh, I don't know."

"I do." Mr Peking was adamant. "And besides, living with a man she's not married to! What will Miss Rogerson think of that?"

"I don't know; but it's not exactly criminal, is it? Nobody thinks anything of it nowadays; it's accepted."

"And it should not be." Mr Peking's heavy face registered massive disapproval, some of which Grant felt was aimed directly at him. "All this permissiveness is at the root of many of the ills of modern society. It's a disease, and until we root it out and return to a more moral way of life we're going to be in trouble. By Jupiter, we are."

"If everybody was utterly moral," Grant said, "you and I would be out of business."

Mr Peking looked at him coldly. "I don't think we need go into that," he said. "What do you know about this Kurt Muller?"

"Not very much."

"How did she get mixed up with him?"

"Quite by chance. It seems she and some friends found him being attacked by two or three young thugs. The thugs ran off and the others helped Muller back to the room where he was living. Everything appears to have started from there."

According to Miss Donson's account of the incident, it had happened rather late at night when she and Angela Harka, together with some other girls and young men, were returning from a party. They were walking because it was a fine night and they felt that a breath of fresh air would be good for them. They had just come to a narrow alleyway when they heard a cry which sounded like a call for help, so they all went into the alleyway and could see what looked like a man lying on the ground with some others standing over him and putting the boot in. They shouted, and the attackers took fright and ran away down the alley, leaving the victim where he was.

It was fortunate for Muller that help came when it did, otherwise he might have been badly injured. As it was he just had some bruises where the men had kicked him and a gash on his forehead. Miss Donson suggested they should call the police, but he seemed very much opposed to this idea, and it would have been pretty useless anyway. He said he had not been robbed; the thugs had not had time. He thanked them for their help and said he would be quite all right now because he had a room not far away; but Angela, who seemed to have been attracted to him straightaway, insisted that they should see he got there safely. With some apparent reluctance he agreed to this, and they all went with him.

The room was on the first floor of an old terrace house, and Angela and Miss Donson and one of the men went up with him to make sure he really was all right. It was not much of a room; Muller told them he had not been living there long and he hoped eventually to get something better. Angela asked him if he would like someone to call a doctor, but he seemed as much against that as he had been against bringing in the police. In fact he seemed to be rather keen to be left to himself, and after a few minutes they all went away. They could hear him locking his door before they got to the stairs.

Angela Harka went back next day to see how he was getting on. He seemed at first disinclined to let her into the room, but finally he did so, and after a while he became more relaxed and even friendly.

Miss Donson said things progressed very fast after that. Angela had obviously fallen for Muller right from the start, and whether he was in love with her or not, he appeared to be willing enough to go along with it. He was maybe ten years or so older than she was, but he had plenty of masculine charm. Within a couple of weeks Angela told Miss Donson she would be leaving the flat; she said she had taken a furnished maisonette, and she and Kurt were going to move into it. She said she was sorry to leave Carol in the lurch, as it were, but for her Kurt was something really special and it just had to be that way.

Grant asked Miss Donson what Muller was doing in England, what he did for a living, but she said she had no idea. And she was not at all sure that Angela knew either – or cared. It seemed to be enough for her just to be with him. She had taken him on trust and seemed to be perfectly happy that it should be that way.

"I don't like it at all," Mr Peking said. "To me it has a very nasty taste. I think that young lady is being most unwise."

"Well, it's her life and there's nothing we can do about it. Are you going to report to Miss Rogerson or do you want me to do it?"

"Neither, for the present. We'll wait until there's rather more to report."

"And meanwhile?"

"Meanwhile," Mr Peking said, "you will find out all you can about this German. He could be a bad lot, you know."

"We have no reason to suppose he is. Miss Donson says he's very charming."

Mr Peking's expression might have suggested that he had just taken a large bite out of a particularly sour lemon.

"That," he said, "doesn't reassure me in the least. Some of the most charming men are the biggest rogues in the business. You had better start making inquiries without delay."

*

Grant decided to pay another call on Miss Donson, and he went round to the basement flat directly after leaving the agency office. It was about eleven o'clock when he got there, and he was doubtful whether he would find her in, but he had to wait only a few seconds after ringing the bell before she opened the door.

"Oh," she said, "it's you again." It was not the warmest

of welcomes, but it was not frigid either; her tone was strictly neutral.

"Yes," Grant said, "it's me again. If you're not too busy I'd like to have another talk."

She gave an odd sort of laugh and said: "Oh, I'm not too busy; far from it. You'd better come in." She led him into the sitting-room and then said: "I was just making some coffee. I suppose you wouldn't care for a cup?"

Grant accepted the offer and she left him sitting in the same armchair he had occupied the previous day while she went away to finish making the coffee. She was back in less than a couple of minutes with two large cups and a plate of biscuits on a tray.

"I didn't really expect you'd be in," Grant said, "but I thought I'd take a chance. Are you having a day off or something?"

She gave another of those odd sort of laughs. "Yes, I'm taking a day off. In fact, if you'd like to know, I've been taking a lot of days off lately, because I happen to have lost my job. The firm I worked for have been rationalising the staff situation; that's the jargon they use. In plain English it means giving a few people the push."

"I'm sorry. What kind of job was it?"

"Secretarial. Nothing grand. But it was a living. Now I'm one of the army of the unemployed."

"I expect you'll soon get something else."

"Ha!" she said. "You may think so. But I can tell you it's not so easy. And of course it comes at an awkward time, because now that Angela has left there's no one to help pay the rent. If something doesn't turn up soon I'm afraid I shall have to start looking for cheaper quarters – a bed-sitter or something of that kind."

"That wouldn't be as nice as this."

"I know it wouldn't, but one has to bow to the force of circumstances."

"Have you tried to find someone else to share this flat?"

"Oh, yes. There've been a few applicants but nobody I'd care to live with. You have to be a bit careful, you know."

"Yes, I suppose so."

"But you didn't come here to listen to my troubles. What's on your mind?"

"Kurt Muller," Grant said.

"Ah, so you're still working on that one."

"Yes, I'm still working on that one. I'd like to know a bit more about him."

"Well, I've told you all I know."

"And what's your honest opinion of him?"

"I think he's very pleasant, good-looking —"

"That isn't quite what I meant."

"So what did you mean?"

"Would you say he's on the level?"

"Why shouldn't he be?"

"No reason. But there are some very dodgy characters around."

"So you think he's dodgy?"

"I don't know. That's the problem; I know very little about him. I just wonder what he's doing in England."

"He's living with Angela, that's what."

Grant smiled. "It's not exactly a career, is it?" He nibbled a biscuit and drank some coffee. "I wonder whether you would do something for me."

"That depends," she said, "on what the something is. You'd better tell me what you want me to do."

"Introduce me to Kurt Muller."

She thought about it. Then: "I suppose that would be possible. But what would I introduce you as — a private eye?"

"No; that isn't quite what I had in mind."

"I didn't think it was." She gave him a pretty shrewd

look. "What you're asking me to do is pass you off as a friend, isn't it?"

"Something like that."

"Angela knows all my friends."

"I could be a new one."

One of her eyebrows lifted. "And what kind of effect on my reputation do you think that would have?"

"Don't you think I'm presentable?"

She cocked her head on one side and looked at him as though giving the question her full consideration. Then she said: "Yes, I suppose you are. You even have a certain rugged charm about you. Are you married, Sam?"

"No."

"Living with anyone?"

"Not at the moment."

"How old are you?"

"Now what is all this? A cross-examination? Do you think I'm too old to be seen around with?"

She laughed. "Now you're being touchy. You're over thirty, aren't you?"

"Yes, I'm over thirty."

"That's what the trouble is with you. You have a nagging fear that you may be over the hill. It saps your self-confidence."

"I thought you were a secretary, not a psychologist," Grant said. "And if you'd like to know, I haven't the slightest fear that I may be over the hill." But he was not really so sure about it. Maybe there was a grain of truth in what she had said; a nasty galling grain.

"You don't have to get angry, Sam."

"I'm not getting angry."

"Very well, you're not getting angry."

"So you're not going to help me?"

"What's in it for me?"

He wondered for a moment whether she was asking for a fee, but then he saw the hint of laughter in her eyes and decided that she was not.

"Suppose I were to take you out to lunch. Would that be sufficient reward?"

"It'll do for a start," she said.

*

They ate at a little restaurant in Soho. Miss Donson had a healthy appetite and did full justice to the meal. In spite of what she had said, she seemed to have no misgivings about being seen around with a man of Grant's advanced age, and he guessed that she had merely been ribbing him.

"I think the best time to go round to Angela's place would be this evening," she said.

"That leaves the afternoon to get through. Do you want me to take you back to your flat?"

"Have you got work to do?"

"Not really. At the moment my work goes by the name of Kurt Muller."

"Would it bore you horribly to go to the Tate and look at an exhibition of modern art?"

"I think I could endure it."

"Right then," she said. "Let's go."

He was not much taken with the modern art but he enjoyed her company, and there were always the Turners to look at if you wanted to see what paint could be made to do under the hands of a genius. The afternoon passed remarkably quickly, and when he suggested going somewhere for tea Miss Donson surprised him by saying that what she would really like would be to see where he lived. He guessed that what she wanted was to do a bit of checking-up on her own account.

"It's nothing much, you know. Just a rather dingy little flat in Camden Town."

"All the same, I'd like to see it."

So he drove her to Camden Town and took her up to the second floor of the old Victorian house which had been carved up into so-called flats. And then he unlocked the door and pushed it open and invited her in. He watched her as she looked at the living-room and tried to see it through her eyes, and he had to admit that it was not very impressive.

"So," she said after a while, "this is where you hang out."

"When I'm at home. There's a kitchenette through there, a bedroom through there and a bathroom through there. I told you it was dingy."

"It could be worse," she said.

"It could be a lot better too," Grant said.

And it had been better when Susan Sims had been sharing it with him; she had certainly brightened up the place. But Miss Sims was no longer around; and she never would be around any more, because all that remained of her was lying six feet under the ground in a Nottingham graveyard. He had missed her a lot at first, but now he seldom thought about her. Sometimes he had a feeling of guilt about that, but it was natural after all: you could not stay in mourning for ever, however much a person might have meant to you when alive.

Carol Donson was inspecting the kitchenette. "There's a lot of dirty crockery in here," she said. "How long do you let it pile up before you do something about it?"

"It varies. Sometimes I have a spell of tidiness when I keep everything spick-and-span, but then I fall from grace and tend to let it all slide. I'm afraid you've caught me in one of the slack periods."

She was taking off her coat. "In that case I think the first thing to do is wash up, don't you?"

"But there's no need for you to —"

"Look," she said, "if we're going to have tea here we shall at least need some clean cups and plates. So let's get moving, shall we?"

It was the first he had heard of their having tea there, but it sounded like a good idea, so he raised no objection. Maybe she even liked washing up. And certainly she seemed to have a gift for culinary organisation: in a very short time she had the kitchenette looking quite presentable. It also looked all the better for having her in it, and he wondered whether, now that she was out of work, she might be persuaded to take on the job of daily help. But he did not suggest it.

Fortunately, the refrigerator was well stocked and they were able to have a satisfying if slightly unorthodox meal. Again Miss Donson exhibited a very healthy appetite and seemed to have no worries about the calorie content of the food she was consuming. Not that she looked as though she had any cause for worry, for though nobody could honestly have described her as sylph-like, she was certainly not overweight. For his money she was just about right.

When the meal was over she suggested that it was time to go and see Muller. Grant held her coat for her, and when she had put her arms into the sleeves he pressed his lips to the side of her neck just below the left ear. She turned slowly and looked at him.

"Now why did you do that?" she asked.

"I don't know. It just seemed like a good thing to do. Have I offended you?"

"You're taking an awful risk, Sam. I might refuse to take you to Angela's place and just tell you to go to hell. You wouldn't like that, would you?"

"Is that what you're going to do?"

"Now I've really got you worried, haven't I?"

"Yes, you've really got me worried."

"You should control your animal instincts."

"Suppose I were to promise to do so in the future. Would that satisfy you?"

She stood for a few moments just looking steadily at him. Then she said: "I'm not sure, Sam, that it would."

It was a somewhat ambiguous answer, but she did not enlarge on it; she simply turned away from him and began to fasten her coat. Grant waited, saying nothing. Maybe he had indeed offended her, and maybe she was going to walk out and leave him to his own devices. He watched her complete the fastening of the coat and then put the knitted woollen hat on her head, all of which she did with great deliberation. Only when she had finished this operation and had pulled on a pair of fleece-lined gloves did she turn and face him again.

"Well?" she said. "Don't you think we had better be going? Or have you changed your mind?"

*

The maisonette was in a narrow road to the north of Clapham Common. It was very small, but the rent even for a place like that could be pretty steep these days, so Grant surmised that Miss Harka's unearned income must be rather higher than Miss Rogerson had led him to suppose. Unless she was digging into her capital or getting some financial help from Muller.

"They may not be in, of course," Miss Donson said. But she rang the bell, which was the chiming kind, and within fifteen seconds the door was opened by a blonde girl whom Grant had no difficulty in recognising from the photograph of Angela Harka.

She seemed delighted to see Miss Donson; she welcomed

her effusively and then shot a glance at Grant. Miss Donson introduced him.

"This is Sam Grant. I wanted you to meet him."

Miss Harka looked at Grant, and he could guess that all kinds of questions were jostling one another in her mind; but she asked none of them. She just said: "Well, come in, both of you."

They went in. There was a midget-sized entrance hall and a sitting-room on the right. Muller was in the sitting-room and he stood up when Miss Harka showed the visitors in. He was just about what Grant had expected from Miss Donson's description – rather less than six feet tall, lean, fair-haired, and quite good-looking if you liked that particular type.

Miss Harka was making the introduction but Grant was not really listening; he was observing Muller's reactions. Muller looked at him, and Grant sensed immediate suspicion, apprehension, perhaps even a hint of fear; all this no more than momentary before Muller's self-control took over and he said smoothly:

"I am very pleased to meet you, Mr Grant."

Grant did not believe a word of it.

7

CRIME OF PASSION

Kohler picked up his luggage at the railway station and went to the address that Herman had given him. It was a rather shabby-looking house in one of the older parts of the town. Kohler took a taxi for some of the way, then paid the driver and walked, carrying his suitcase in his hand.

A skinny, sharp-featured man with eyes as beady as a rodent's opened the door. He had lank, greasy black hair plastered thinly over his scalp and a growth of dark stubble shading cheeks and chin. The brown suit he was wearing hung loosely on his meagre frame and had the look of something that had been picked up in a second-hand clothes store.

"Yes?" he said, peering suspiciously at Kohler.

"I am looking for a man named Steiner," Kohler said.

"I am Steiner."

"My name is Kohler. I was told to –"

Steiner glanced quickly up and down the street, then shot out a hand and grabbed Kohler's sleeve. "Come in, come in. Don't stand there. Come inside."

Kohler went in and Steiner closed the door. They were in a narrow hallway smelling faintly of dry-rot, and Kohler could see a flight of stairs with a passage on the left-hand side leading to a door with frosted-glass panels in the upper half.

"You were expecting me?" he asked.

Steiner ignored the question. "Follow me," he said, and began to climb the stairs.

The house had three storeys and they went up to the top floor. Steiner showed Kohler into a room with a dormer window. There was linoleum on the floor and a single-bed was pushed up against the wall on the right. The rest of the furniture consisted of a wardrobe, a dressing-table and a chair. On the dressing-table was a small pile of paperback books. For heating there was a tarnished electric fire, but it was not switched on and the room was chilly.

Kohler put his suitcase on the bed and cast a glance of some distaste at his surroundings, reflecting that he had made a poor exchange for the comparative luxury of Gerda Vogel's comfortable flat.

"How long am I to stay here?" he asked.

Steiner's thin shoulders lifted slightly. "That is not for me to decide. But while you are here it will be best if you do not leave the house. In fact, those are orders. There is a bathroom on the other side of the landing. Your meals will be brought up to you. Good?"

Kohler thought it was very far from good, but he had to accept the situation. He was a pawn and somebody else was dictating his moves. It was galling but unavoidable; and at least it was better than falling into the hands of the police.

Steiner went away and Kohler switched on the electric fire. He looked out of the window and had a view of the other side of the road. He left the window very quickly, having a feeling that somebody might be spying on him from one of those blank windows across the way. He felt like a prisoner in that small attic room and he hoped he would not have to be there for long. He would have liked to be back in East Germany, where he would have felt safe;

but apparently that was not to be. He wondered uneasily where they were planning to send him and on what mission. His mind was plagued by this uncertainty regarding his future and he was afraid.

Later in the day Steiner himself brought a meal. He tried to engage Steiner in conversation but the man was having none of it; he was cold and taciturn and unfriendly. He did not stay to watch Kohler eat the meal but he came back after half an hour to collect the tray. After that Kohler had the room to himself again.

He glanced at the books but there was nothing he wanted to read. He lay on the bed, staring at the ceiling and remembering that last evening in Gerda Vogel's flat; remembering how long it had taken to kill her and what a messy business it had been. He had no remorse, just a feeling of dissatisfaction for not having completed the task with more expertise. It was damaging to his self-esteem to recall how inexpert and even panicky he had been. Herman had not troubled to disguise his contempt when he had been told of the way in which his order had been carried out.

Occasionally he heard noises in the house; doors being closed, muffled voices, footsteps on the stairs and the first floor landing. But no one came up to the top floor; no one but Steiner. He went to the bathroom, which was a cramped little room with an old stained bath and a chain-operated lavatory cistern. When it grew dark he drew the curtain across the dormer window and switched the light on.

At eight o'clock in the evening Steiner brought him his last meal of the day. Kohler asked if there was any news.

"No," Steiner said. "What news should there be?"

"About me. About what is to happen to me."

"That is no concern of mine," Steiner said.

Kohler went to bed early; there was nothing else to do.

The mattress was lumpy and he did not sleep well although he was tired. When he went to the bathroom in the morning he found that there was no hot water. Nor was there a socket for his electric shaver. When Steiner brought him his breakfast Kohler asked whether he could find an adaptor so that he could use the socket which the electric fire was plugged into.

"Why don't you use an ordinary razor?" Steiner said.

"Because I haven't got one."

Grumblingly, Steiner promised to see what he could do, and an hour later he came back with an adaptor.

"Thank you," Kohler said. "Do you think I could see a newspaper?"

Steiner shook his head. "What do you want with a newspaper?"

"I want to read it, of course."

Steiner pointed at the books on the dressing-table. "If you want to read, read those." Without waiting for any argument he turned and left the room.

Kohler wondered whether Steiner was simply being obstructive or whether he had had instructions not to allow his guest to have access to the news. There was no radio either, so he had no means of telling whether Gerda Vogel's body had been discovered. Well, perhaps it was better not to know, since he could do nothing about it, and it would only worry him if he were to know that the police were looking for him. Not that ignorance saved him from worrying; far from it. In fact he even worried about not knowing whether there was yet any cause for worry.

Five days passed and it seemed like a year. The feeling of being a prisoner in the room never left him; he knew every crack in the ceiling, every patch of discoloration in the wallpaper, every mark of wear on the linoleum. He dreamed about Gerda Vogel, saw her bruised face and bloodstained body floating towards him, following him with outstretched arms, inviting him to make love to her. He woke bathed in sweat and wondered whether he was going mad.

The sixth night he awoke to find that the light had been switched on. A man was bending over him, touching his shoulder with one hand and peering into his face.

"Well, Kohler?" the man said. "How are you feeling?"

He stared up at the man and saw that it was Herman. He struggled to sit up in the bed and looked at his watch. It was one o'clock in the morning. He could not understand why Herman should have come to see him at that hour.

"You!" he said. "Why are you here?"

"I have come to give you your orders."

"At this hour of the night!"

"It is better that I should come at night – for obvious reasons." Herman stood away from the bed; he was wearing the leather coat in which Kohler had last seen him. "In three hours from now you are to leave this house. A car will come for you. See that you are ready."

Kohler got out of bed and shivered. The electric fire was switched off and the room had become icily cold. He switched it on and began to dress; there was no point in trying to get any more sleep if he was to leave so soon.

"Where shall I be going?"

"To Hamburg."

"And then?"

"You will receive further instructions when you get there."

Kohler pulled up the zipper of his trousers. "What has been happening? Has the –"

"The body of Gerda Vogel," Herman said, "was discovered on the day you left the flat. When she did not arrive for work someone at the office telephoned the flat and got no answer. They wondered whether she was ill or had had an accident and was unable to reach the telephone. The rest was inevitable."

"And the police?"

"They are looking for a man who is known to have been living with her. Fortunately, of course, the murder is being regarded as a crime of passion. No political motive is suspected. Certainly the manner in which it was carried out would scarcely have suggested anything but a man killing his mistress while in a state of complete frenzy. Wouldn't you agree?" Herman's tone was acid, a trifle sarcastic.

Kohler made no answer. He wondered just how Herman would have acted in a similar situation. Perhaps he would have used poison; he looked like a poisoner.

"Incidentally," Herman said, "you will be travelling to Hamburg as Oskar Braun, a free-lance journalist from Munster. It is unlikely that you will be called upon to identify yourself but if it should be necessary these ought to be sufficient." He handed Kohler a driving licence and a credit card, both giving the appearance of having been well used and both made out in the name of Oskar Braun. Kohler took the documents and stowed them in an inner pocket of his jacket.

"I think that is all," Herman said. "I shall leave now. It is probable that we shall not meet again."

He did not offer to shake hands, did not wish Kohler good luck, did not even say farewell; he merely turned and left the room. He must have gone down the stairs very silently, for Kohler heard no sound of his descent. Nor did he hear a door closing as Herman left the house, nor any sound of a car starting up; Herman had probably taken the precaution of leaving his car some distance away and approaching the house on foot.

Kohler went to the bathroom and then shaved. He packed his suitcase, lit a cigarette and sat down to wait. It

was about twenty minutes past three when he heard
someone coming up the stairs. There was a knock on the
door and Steiner came in with a tray on which were a cup of
coffee and a plate of sandwiches. Kohler was surprised at so
much thoughtfulness on Steiner's part, and thanked him.

"No telling when you'll get breakfast," Steiner said
gruffly. He seemed slightly embarrassed by Kohler's
thanks. He was fully dressed and Kohler wondered whether
he had been to bed. Perhaps he slept in his clothes.

There was a nervous flutter in Kohler's stomach. What
lay ahead of him was wrapped in mystery; all he knew was
that he was to be taken to Hamburg, but after that, what
more? It was no use asking Steiner; even if he knew – and it
was pretty well certain that he did not – he would not be
likely to tell; he was the kind of man who believed in
keeping a still tongue in his head. He did not linger to chat
with Kohler, but having delivered the tray, left the room
almost immediately.

At five minutes to four he came to report that the car had
arrived and that it was time for Kohler to leave. Kohler put
on his raincoat and hat, picked up the suitcase and followed
Steiner down the stairs.

There was a man waiting in the hall. He was a youngish,
thick-set individual with short fair hair and a snub nose. He
was wearing gold-rimmed glasses and a black quilted rally
coat. He introduced himself:

"Franz Richter."

"Oskar Braun," Kohler said.

Richter smiled. It was probable that he knew this was
not Kohler's real name, but he made no remark. Steiner
opened the door; he seemed to be impatient to be rid of
them and there was no reason for lingering.

The car was a grey BMW. Richter opened the boot and
put Kohler's suitcase inside. There was already a brown
leather or plastic holdall in the boot, which Kohler

supposed was Richter's. Richter closed the boot and they got into the car. Kohler glanced back at the house and saw that the door was shut and that there was no sign of Steiner. That was another man he did not expect ever to meet again.

Richter started the engine and the BMW got smoothly away. Long before daylight they were clear of Bonn and were on the autobahn heading north towards Munster. Richter did not talk much but concentrated on his driving. Kohler found himself falling asleep for brief spells and then waking up again to discover that nothing had changed and that the BMW was still pressing steadily on. Then, after a rather longer nap, he woke to find that Richter had stopped the car at a motorway restaurant. He glanced at his watch; it was coming up to a quarter to eight on a dull, damp morning; his mouth felt dry and he had a slight headache.

"We eat here," Richter said. "Hungry?"

"Yes," Kohler said. He had eaten only two of Steiner's sandwiches and he was ready for breakfast. He followed Richter out of the car and into the restaurant.

Kohler felt much better when they returned to the car. Richter bought some petrol and they got under way again. It had begun to rain and the windscreen-wipers had to be brought into action. Kohler wondered how much Richter knew about him; did he know that he was acting as chauffeur to a man who had killed a woman and was wanted by the police? The question bothered Kohler a little, but he did not ask Richter.

Twenty-five kilometres north of Minden they ran into a roadblock. There was a queue of vehicles waiting to go through, and armed police seemed to be present in force. Kohler's pulse began to hammer and his mouth felt dry again.

"Turn back," he said.

Richter told him sharply not to be a fool. "How can I turn back? It is impossible."

Kohler put a hand on the door-catch with some wild idea of making a run for it, but Richter gripped his arm and held him down in the seat.

"Stay where you are. Have you gone mad?"

"But the police will get me."

"How do you know it's you they're interested in?"

"It's certain."

"It is not certain, but it will be if you try to run away. Keep calm."

Kohler took his hand off the door. Richter was right, of course; nothing could be more incriminating than an attempt to escape. But as the car moved spasmodically forward in the queue he found it impossible to take the matter as calmly as Richter appeared to be doing. Richter, however, was not wanted for murder, and that made a difference; it made all the difference in the world.

A policeman came to the door of the car, and there was another behind him with a submachine-gun slung from his right shoulder, his eyes watchful and suspicious. Richter lowered the window.

"What's the trouble?"

The policeman did not say what the trouble was. He said: "Your driving licence, please."

Richter produced his licence and the policeman examined it.

"Where have you come from?"

"From Munster," Richter said.

"And you are going where?"

"Hamburg."

The policeman handed back the driving licence and looked past him at Kohler. His eyes were ice-blue, his face expressionless. Kohler had already pulled out the driving licence that Herman had given him, though the policeman had not asked for it. Perhaps it was a mistake, that over-eagerness to produce documentary evidence of identification; perhaps he should have waited, playing it cool. The policeman took the licence, glanced at it and then at Kohler.

"You are Oskar Braun?"

"Yes."

"You have also come from Munster?"

"Yes."

"And are going to Hamburg?"

"Yes."

The policeman handed back the licence and spoke to Richter. "I must ask you to open the boot."

Richter got out of the car and Kohler did so also; he felt too much on edge just to sit and wait. It was still raining, but only lightly. Behind the BMW a long line of vehicles stretched back along the autobahn, but the police were not hurrying; they had a job to do and they meant to do it thoroughly. Richter opened the boot and the policeman looked at the suitcase and the holdall.

"Open the bags."

Richter opened the holdall and the policeman rummaged in it but found nothing incriminating. Richter stepped aside and allowed Kohler to open the suitcase. It contained nothing to arouse suspicion. The policeman appeared satisfied. Richter closed the boot and he and Kohler got back into the car. Richter leaned out of the window and spoke to the policeman.

"What are you looking for?"

The policeman made a signal with his hand. "Get moving."

Some time later they heard a news item on the car radio. Terrorists had ambushed a prominent Hanover businessman named Artur Schneider, head of a large manufacturing combine, as he was being driven to his office in a black Mercedes. The terrorists had riddled the car with bullets from automatic weapons, killing Herr Schneider, his driver and a young female secretary who was travelling with them. Police over a wide area were engaged in hunting the killers but no arrests had yet been made.

Richter switched off the radio. "And you wanted to run away."

"I didn't know, did I?" Kohler said. He felt nettled by Richter's tone. It had been only natural to suppose that the police were looking for him, only natural to be alarmed. He knew now that there had been no cause for alarm, but at the time there had been no way of knowing; the policeman had not been giving anything away. "They could have been looking for me."

Richter cast a slightly mocking glance at him. "What makes you think you're that important?"

Again Kohler felt nettled. What right had Richter to be so contemptuous? Was he himself so important? He turned away from Richter and watched the traffic flashing past on the other side of the autobahn. He thought he heard Richter give a faint snigger but he ignored it. He wondered gloomily what orders he would receive in Hamburg.

8

CRAZY POLAK

It was a fair-sized modern house in a pleasant residential part of Hamburg. It was the kind of house a reasonably prosperous businessman might have lived in – and for all Kohler knew to the contrary, possibly did. There were a lot of other houses, all standing well back from the road, all of comparatively recent construction and all with that same air of unostentatious prosperity.

It was a little after midday when they arrived and it had stopped raining. Richter parked the BMW at the side of the house and he and Kohler got out. Richter opened the boot and lifted out his holdall.

"Take your suitcase," he said.

Kohler took the suitcase and Richter closed the boot. He led the way round to the front door but there was no need to ring the bell, for the door opened as soon as they reached it and a dark-haired, well-dressed man who might have been aged about fifty invited them to step inside. They went in and the warmth of the house enveloped them like a cloak. The dark-haired man closed the door; from his appearance he could have been that reasonably prosperous businessman who might have owned the house. He had a light tenor voice which seemed to go well with his rather slight build.

"Let me introduce myself. I am Helmut Bloch. You may leave your luggage here for the present."

They put their bags down on the floor and Richter said: "I am Franz Richter."

"I had already guessed so," Bloch said. "I was looking out of the window when you arrived and I saw you driving the car." He turned to Kohler. "For the moment I suppose I should call you Herr Braun."

"As you wish," Kohler said. "The name is not important."

"You have had a pleasant journey? No incidents?"

"We ran into a police checkpoint," Richter said. "I think they were looking for terrorists, but Herr Braun wanted to run away."

Kohler shot him a venomous glance. Richter was laughing at him again and inviting Bloch to share the joke. But Bloch did not smile.

"That would have been a foolish thing to do," he said. He looked at Kohler and his face had hardened. "A very foolish thing indeed."

There was a steeliness in Bloch's eyes and in his voice, which was in contrast to his former easy manner. Kohler shifted from one foot to the other, unable to meet Bloch's gaze.

"Well, I didn't do it."

"I persuaded him it would be unwise," Richter said. "I had to twist his arm but I persuaded him."

Kohler turned on him. "All right, so you persuaded me. Now can we forget it?" He spoke to Bloch. "How long shall I be staying here?"

"Your stay," Bloch said, "will be very brief. Come this way."

They followed him into a large sitting-room with windows looking out on to a well-kept lawn. There was a man already in the room, a broad-shouldered individual with a stack of untidy hair in which flecks of grey were beginning to mingle with the darker colour. He had a beetling forehead and thick eyebrows meeting above the bridge of his nose. Bloch introduced him as Conrad Franke.

Franke grinned at Kohler and offered a large blunt hand to shake. Kohler could feel the strength in it, and the thought flickered into his mind that a man with hands such as this could have broken Gerda Vogel's neck with ease and would not have had to resort to the knife. He wondered where Franke fitted into the picture, but nobody offered any information on that point and he did not ask.

After a few desultory exchanges on topics of a neutral nature conversation seemed to hang fire and Kohler was not sorry when a very fat middle-aged woman came to announce that lunch was ready.

The dining-room was at the rear of the house, and the fat woman, who might have been cook and general housekeeper, waited on them but said very little. The conversation that had flagged in the sitting-room showed little sign of revival over the meal. Kohler supposed that sooner or later he would be told where he was going and what was expected of him and that he would simply have to be patient.

When the meal was finished Bloch pushed his chair back and stood up. He spoke to Kohler.

"You may as well change your clothes now. Then you will be ready."

"Ready for what?" Kohler asked.

"To leave. As I told you, you will not be staying here for long."

"Why must I change my clothes?"

"It will not be only your clothes you will be changing," Bloch told him. "You will also be changing your identity. Come."

Kohler followed Bloch out of the dining-room and up the

stairs to a bedroom. Franke accompanied them but not Richter. Kohler got the impression that having transported him from Bonn to Hamburg, Richter's interest in him was now at an end; possibly he would stay the night at the house and return to Bonn next day.

There was a double-bed in the room and on the bed a pair of dark blue serge trousers, a blue roll-neck pullover and a grey tweed jacket were laid out. None of the items was new, and the jacket in particular had obviously had a good deal of wear.

"Take off your suit and tie," Bloch said, "and put these on. You may keep your own underclothing and shoes."

Kohler did as he was instructed. The jacket and trousers were not a perfect fit; the man who had previously worn them had apparently been an inch or two larger in the waist than Kohler and his shoulders had been slightly wider; but Bloch appeared satisfied with the result.

"Yes," he said, having inspected Kohler from all sides like an assistant in a ready-made clothes shop, "that will be all right, I think." He glanced at Franke. "What do you say?"

"Oh, he'll do well enough," Franke said. "They'll hardly look at him anyway. And with the coat and the cap on –"

A black gaberdine trenchcoat was draped over the back of a chair and on the seat was a navy blue peaked cap. Bloch walked over to the dressing-table and picked up a leather wallet, which he handed to Kohler.

"Look inside."

Kohler opened the wallet and saw that it contained some money and a printed document which appeared to be a seaman's shore pass. It bore an official stamp and the name of a ship – the "Josef Pulaski". What surprised Kohler a little was the fact that, though the seaman's name on the pass was Jan Rakowski, the photograph that was attached to it was of himself. And yet he should not have been surprised; there had been ample time during his stay at the house in Bonn for this kind of business to be attended to.

"So," he said, "I am now Jan Rakowski."

Bloch nodded. "Polish ship's steward."

"But I do not speak Polish."

"There will be no need to."

"When do I join my ship?"

"This evening."

"And have you any other instructions for me?"

"None," Bloch said. "You understand of course that you will leave your suitcase and this suit here?"

"There are things in the suitcase I should like to keep."

"They are Oskar Braun's – or should I say Hans Kohler's? You are no longer either Braun or Kohler; you are Jan Rakowski. You will leave everything; is that clear?"

Kohler shrugged resignedly. "Yes, quite clear."

He wondered why he was being sent to Poland; there was surely nothing for him to do in that country. But perhaps Poland was only a step on his way back to East Germany; perhaps they were sending him home by the back door. The thought cheered him slightly.

*

The bar was in the docks area. It was crowded with seamen and women of a certain character. The lighting was dim and the air was polluted with tobacco smoke and the reek of beer and spirits and human sweat.

"What will you drink?" Franke asked.

"Nothing," Kohler said. He did not feel like drinking. He was wearing the black trenchcoat and the blue peaked cap and he felt ill-at-ease in the strange clothes.

"Do you wish to make yourself conspicuous?" Franke said. "You must have something."

"Very well then; a beer."

Franke bought two mugs of beer and let his gaze travel round the room. Then he gave a kind of grunt of satisfaction and said: "Follow me."

The man he had spotted was sitting in a corner and smoking a short fat cigar; there was a glass of pale liquid on the table in front of him which might have been gin or vodka. There were two vacant chairs at the table; Franke sat down on one and indicated that Kohler should take the other. They put the beer mugs on the table and Franke looked at the man with the cigar.

"Good evening, Herr Nowak."

The man he had called Nowak gave a slight nod but said nothing. He was wearing a quilted parka and a red woollen cap with a tassle on the top. The hair which came straggling down from under the cap was so pale in colour that it was almost silver and his face was thin and narrow. He had a small moustache and looked about thirty years old.

"This," Franke said, resting a hand on Kohler's shoulder, "is your man."

Nowak looked at Kohler, squinting through the smoke that curled upward from the cigar between his lips. Then he nodded again, took the cigar from his mouth and said in good German: "I am glad to make your acquaintance. Though perhaps I should not say that. I am already acquainted with you, no? We are shipmates, you and I; is it not so?" He grinned suddenly, revealing a set of large uneven teeth like a badly erected palisade. "How are you, shipmate?"

"Well enough," Kohler said. He was not sure he cared greatly for the look of Nowak, but he was in no position to pick and choose his companions, so he would have to make the best of things as they were. "When do we go on board?"

"Later."

"Why not now?" Kohler had no desire to spend an evening drinking with Nowak.

"Nobody goes back to his ship this early," Nowak said. "It would look odd. Best to wait. Why be in such a hurry? Don't you like it here?"

Kohler shrugged. "Whatever you say."

Franke drained his beer mug and stood up. "I leave you now." He touched Kohler's arm. "You do what Herr Nowak tells you and you'll be all right."

Kohler had some doubts about that but he said nothing. Franke gave a nod to Nowak and walked away; his part in the operation, like Richter's, was finished.

"My first name," Nowak said, "is Stefan. I will call you Jan. For the present you must get used to that, you understand?"

"I understand." Did Nowak think he was a child that he needed to have this explained to him?

"You look sad, Jan. What you need is a real drink, not that beer. Wait here. I get you a vodka."

Kohler started to say he wanted no spirits, but Nowak was already on his way. He decided to drink just one glass of vodka and no more, but when Nowak came back it was obvious that he was looking forward to a longer session and was going to take it as great incivility if Kohler did not keep his end up. Kohler resigned himself to it; he was entirely dependent on Nowak to lead him to the ship and had to stick with him.

After two or three vodkas Kohler was beginning to feel somewhat happier; there was a warm glow inside him and a sense of overall well-being. It occurred to him that perhaps Nowak was not such a bad fellow after all.

Nowak observed the change in Kohler. "I was right, no? You are feeling better now?"

"Yes," Kohler said. "Much better." Nevertheless, there

was a small voice inside his head warning him to take care;
it would not be wise to get drunk; he must keep his wits
about him because he was not yet out of the wood by a long
way.

Nowak emptied his glass. "And now," he said, "I think
we have one more drink and then we find ourselves two
women." He grinned at Kohler, again baring those ugly
teeth of his. "What do you say, Jan?"

Alarm flickered up in Kohler, sobering him. "No; it
would not be advisable. I don't think –"

Nowak leaned over and rested a hand on his arm. "What
are you afraid of? There is no danger. Tomorrow we are at
sea. No women then. Last chance, Jan, last chance."

He bought the final drink and Kohler's alarm subsided.
Maybe Nowak was right; what danger was there in it? It
might be far less dangerous than staying where they were
and getting more and more drunk.

Nowak set his empty glass down. "All right, Jan?"

"All right, Stefan," Kohler said.

*

Kohler's woman was a blonde, about thirty years old.
When she had taken off her clothes there seemed to be a lot
of her; she was built on a generous Germanic scale like a
prima donna in one of Wagner's operas. Nowak's partner
was smaller, dark-haired, slightly younger perhaps. Kohler
could hear them in the adjoining room; the dividing wall
seemed to be paper-thin. There were mysterious rattling
noises and now and then the sound of Nowak's muffled
laughter. He seemed to be enjoying himself.

It was Nowak who had insisted that they should keep
more or less in touch with each other. Kohler had agreed
with that; if he lost contact with Nowak he would be in real
trouble; he needed the Pole to take him on board the "Josef

Pulaski", which was to be his means of escape from the Federal Republic.

Kohler was not enjoying himself as Nowak appeared to be; he was too worried. He was still slightly fuddled by the vodka he had drunk, but the effect was wearing off and it was not enough to allay his misgivings. Maybe it had not after all been wise to let Nowak lead him into this adventure; no good would come of it; early or not, they should have gone straight to the ship.

The blonde naked woman lying beside him seemed to become aware that something was wrong. She touched Kohler's cheek with her fingers.

"You don't look happy, dear."

"I'm not happy," Kohler said.

She pressed closer to him and he could feel all that soft pliant flesh moulding itself into contact with his own harder body. He could feel the warmth of her and smell the mingling odours of sweat and perfume that should have roused him but served merely to produce a feeling of disgust and aversion.

"Don't I please you?"

"It has nothing to do with you," Kohler said.

"There's something on your mind, isn't there? You can tell me if you like. I'm a good listener. In a way I'm like a priest." She giggled. "Funny, isn't it? People – men, that is – tell things to me they wouldn't tell their own wives. It seems to do them good, and it's safe; nothing I hear goes any further. So if you'd like to talk about it, dear, you go ahead."

"I don't want to talk about it," Kohler said. He would really have had to be mad to do that. Maybe it was true that she did not repeat things that were told her by her clients; maybe if he told her about the killing of Gerda Vogel she would keep even that to herself; whores preferred to stay away from the police. But he had no intention of telling her; he needed no confessional to ease his mind; all he wanted was to get safely on board the "Josef Pulaski".

"Well," she said, "if that's the way you feel – you please yourself. I'm just trying to help."

"I know. But I don't need help – not that kind." He rolled away from her and got off the bed. He went to his clothes, carefully folded where he had left them on a chair.

"What are you doing?" the woman asked.

"I need a smoke," Kohler said. He felt in the pocket of the jacket and pulled out a packet of cigarettes and a lighter.

"You can give me one," the woman said. She sat up on the bed.

Kohler brought her a cigarette and lit it for her. Her breasts were heavy and sagging and there were a lot of folds in the flesh of her neck. There was a mole on the right-hand side of her chin and she had put so much eye-shadow on that he thought she looked weird. He turned away from her and went back to the chair and began to dress.

"Have you had enough?" she asked, surprised.

"Yes, I've had enough."

"Well, you're a strange one. I thought you wanted to stay longer."

"I'm not going yet. I've got to wait for him." Kohler pointed at the wall on the other side of which they could still hear faint sounds of Nowak enjoying himself.

She gave him an odd look. "You and him are very close friends?"

Kohler shook his head. "I wouldn't say that. I'm not sure we're friends at all."

"I don't understand you."

"You don't have to," Kohler said.

He finished dressing. The blonde women got off the bed and started dressing too.

"So what do we do now?" she asked.

"Just wait. Do you mind?"

"It's crazy," she said. "But you're the one that's paying, so why should I mind? What have I got to lose?" She went to the mirror and began to repair her make-up; and that was when the woman in the adjoining room started screeching. Something was thumping against the other side of the wall between the two rooms, making a kind of accompaniment to the screeches, like a bass drum in a band.

The blonde woman turned her head, the lipstick in her hand arrested half-way to her mouth. "What in hell's going on in there?"

Kohler did not stop to suggest an answer; he was already on his way to the door. As he came out into the corridor a man went past him at a run; a big, tough-looking, bald-headed individual with a lot of scars on his face that might have been made by knives or razors or bits of broken glass. The man got to the door of the room which the screeches were coming from just a step ahead of Kohler, and the blonde woman was no more than three steps behind him. The door was locked, but it was no obstacle to the bald-headed man; he just put his shoulder to it and something gave way with a sharp cracking sound. The man went in without troubling to knock.

There was no need to ask why the dark-haired woman was kicking up such a racket: Nowak had got a grip on her neck and was beating her head against the wall as if he was trying to knock a hole in it. They were both stark naked, and the woman was hitting at Nowak and giving him a scratch or two with her nails, but it was not stopping him, and every now and then she would let out another squeal like a pig having its throat cut.

The bald-headed man went straight for Nowak and clapped a hand on his left shoulder. Until that moment Nowak appeared to have been unaware that there was anyone else in the room besides himself and the dark-haired woman, but when he felt the hand on his shoulder he turned his head and saw the man. He wasted no time in working out the situation; he just let go of the woman with his left hand and made a sideways chop with it, catching the man on the throat. With his clothes on Nowak had not appeared to have much in the way of physique, but stripped to the skin he looked all sinew and muscle, and the way he hit the bald-headed man showed that he knew something about self-defence. The bald-headed man took his hand off Nowak's shoulder and staggered back a pace or two making noises in his throat.

"Why don't you get to hell out of here?" Nowak said. "Can't you see this is a private party?" He was still holding the dark-haired woman pinned to the wall with his right hand, but she had stopped screeching for the moment.

The bald-headed man showed no inclination to act on Nowak's suggestion. He recovered quickly and fished a knife out of his pocket. The knife had a spring blade and he pressed the catch and it shot out like the tongue of a snake. He made a lunge at Nowak, but Nowak was on the alert and he released the woman and swayed to the left. The knife touched him under the lower ribs on his right-hand side, lightly cutting the skin and letting a little blood ooze out, as though someone had drawn a line in red ink.

"Ah!" Nowak said. It was like a faint sigh.

The bald-headed man slashed at his face, but Nowak jerked his head back and the blade passed by within an inch of his eyes. The bald-headed man tried again, and again Nowak dodged. But it could not go on indefinitely like this; Nowak was naked and unarmed, and there was little space for manoeuvre; sooner or later he was going to be caught by the knife.

Kohler understood this very well, and he understood also that if Nowak were to be badly injured his own safety was going to be put in jeopardy; which was a state of things not at all to his liking. If it had not been for this consideration he might have left Nowak to look after himself as best he could; but as matters were he decided, with some reluctance, that he had better take a hand in the game. He looked for a weapon and saw one standing on the dressing-table – an unopened bottle of vodka which Nowak had bought before leaving the bar earlier in the evening. Kohler picked up the bottle by the neck and clubbed the bald-headed man on the back of the cranium.

It was the way he had hit Gerda Vogel that time in the flat in Bonn; but this bottle was stronger and it did not break. The bald-headed man's legs folded as if the bones had turned to rubber and he slumped to the floor.

"Good work," Nowak said. He sounded very cool for a man who had almost had his eyes slashed with a knife. But possibly he had a right to be cool, with no clothes on.

Kohler put the vodka bottle back on the dressing-table and picked up the knife which was lying on the floor. The bald-headed man was not moving. The blonde woman started towards the door, but he got there before her and pushed it shut with his foot. He stood with his back against it, holding the knife in his right hand, the point of the blade extended towards the woman.

"Wait," he said.

She came to a stop, looking scared.

Nowak was getting dressed and was losing no time about it. The dark-haired woman was sitting on the bed, and she also looked scared – too scared to do anything, even to put her clothes on. She had a nice body, Kohler thought; it was well-formed and not so fleshy as the blonde's. He wondered why Nowak had been hammering the wall with her head; there seemed no apparent reason why he should have been dissatisfied with her.

It took Nowak about half a minute to get dressed. When

he had done so he hauled some deutschmarks from his pocket, walked over to the women sitting on the bed, gave her a kiss and pushed the notes down between her thighs as though he had been posting some letters. She did not move, just looked at him. He gave her a playful smack on the buttock.

"Cheer up. It's not the end of the world."

She made no answer. The man on the floor made a movement and gave a loud sigh. He was coming to.

"Let's go," Kohler said.

Nowak picked up the bottle of vodka and pushed the blonde woman out of the way. "Sure thing. Let's go."

Kohler dropped the knife and opened the door. There was no one in the corridor. Ten seconds later they were out of the house and walking rapidly away. No one was following them and there was no sound of any alarm.

"Will they tell the police?" Kohler said.

Nowak gave a laugh. "You bet your life they won't. What good would it do them?"

"What was the trouble? Why were you knocking the woman's brains out?"

"She called me a filthy Polak bastard, that's why."

"What made her call you that?"

"She didn't like something I did."

"What was it?"

"It's none of your damned business," Nowak said.

They continued to walk but gradually slackened the pace. It was a cold night with a chilly breeze blowing, but there was no rain. There was a lot of traffic moving along under the glow of the street-lamps and plenty of people still around.

"Maybe she was about right," Kohler said. "Maybe you are a filthy Polak bastard. And crazy too."

Nowak laughed again. "Maybe I am, but I don't take

that sort of thing from any cheap little whore."

"Not so cheap at that," Kohler said, remembering the deutschmarks. "Now do we go to the ship?"

"Not yet. First we find some nice place to have supper. I'm hungry. I'm always hungry after I have a woman; it gives me an appetite."

Kohler groaned, mentally damning Nowak's appetite and the crazy Polak himself to Hades. But he had to accept this further delay and just hope that Nowak did not start knocking a waiter's head against the wall because of some fancied shortcoming in the service.

*

It was past midnight when they came to the dock entrance, and there was no trouble at all, their passes receiving no more than a cursory glance.

"That's the way it is at this time of night," Nowak said. "Everybody is half asleep. Who's interested in a couple of seamen going back to their ship after an evening on the town?"

Kohler was relieved. It had been bothering him, but in the event there had been nothing to it.

The "Josef Pulaski" was a modern white-painted cargo vessel with hatches covered and derricks secured. They climbed the gang-plank and Nowak conducted Kohler to the cabin they were to share. It was small but looked clean and comfortable. Nowak opened a wardrobe and revealed some clothing.

"This is yours while you are on board. All right?"

"All right," Kohler said. He wondered whether there had been a real Jan Rakowski who had worn these clothes. Perhaps; and perhaps he was now calling himself Oskar Braun or some other name. But it was no concern of his.

"How long will it take us to reach Poland?" he asked.

Nowak grinned at him. "What makes you think we are going to Poland, my friend?"

"But this ship —"

"Will sail in the morning for England," Nowak said. "I thought you knew."

9

ASSIGNMENT

During the short voyage to England Kohler had little
contact with any of the crew of the "Josef Pulaski" except
Stefan Nowak, who appeared to be a genuine ship's
steward. Kohler was relieved to find that he was not
expected to carry out any duties in that line. He spent most
of his time in the cabin, taking only occasional spells on
deck for exercise and fresh air. When Nowak was not
otherwise engaged he practised speaking English with him.
Kohler had learnt English as part of his training in East
Germany, but he had had no call to use it since then and his
command of it had become rather less than perfect. Nowak
was a good linguist and was as fluent in that language as he
was in German; with his help Kohler found himself quickly
picking up the lost threads.

The ship was at sea for one night only and docked at
Ipswich late the following afternoon. It was dark when
Kohler went ashore in company with Nowak. He was
carrying no luggage; Nowak had told him that it would not
be necessary. He was wearing the black trenchcoat and the
blue peaked cap which he had been given by Bloch in
Hamburg.

The car was waiting in a narrow street not far from the
docks. It was a yellow Allegro and there was a man sitting
in the driver's seat.

"Wait here," Nowak said.

He walked up to the car and spoke to the man behind the wheel. Then he came back to where Kohler was standing.

"Everything is in order. This is where you and I part company. It is unlikely we shall meet again. I wish you the best of luck."

"Thank you," Kohler said. Nowak had exasperated him that first night of their acquaintanceship by his reckless actions which seemed likely to lead them into trouble, but now that the time had come to say goodbye to the crazy Polak he was surprised to find that he did so with some regret. "And thank you for your help."

Nowak grinned, giving Kohler a last glimpse of those ugly teeth. "And thank you for your help, too."

Kohler understood that he was referring to that piece of work with the vodka bottle; but Kohler had done it for his own benefit, not Nowak's. Still, there was no need to tell Nowak that. He turned and walked to the yellow car.

The door was open, and he got in and pulled it shut behind him. The man sitting behind the wheel turned his head and looked at him; he had a pale face and a dark, untidy moustache; he was wearing black-rimmed glasses and his hair was receding from a broad, pale forehead.

"Welcome to England," he said in German. Then, switching to English: "I am glad you got here safely. You may call me Carl." He started the engine and got the car moving.

"I suppose you know my name," Kohler said.

"Of course. You are Jan Rakowski – for the present." He chuckled softly, as though the idea amused him.

"Where are we going?" Kohler asked.

"Not far. To a house where you will stay the night."

"And tomorrow?"

"Tomorrow is another day," Carl said.

It was an old red-brick house on the west side of the

town. A sallow-complexioned, dyspeptic-looking man in a sober grey suit opened the door to them and conducted them to a room where another man was sitting in an armchair and reading a magazine. This man put the magazine down and stood up when the others entered, and Kohler saw that he was about the same age and build as himself. The sallow-faced man did not introduce him; nor for that matter did he introduce himself. The other man gave Kohler a brief inspection and appeared to be satisfied with what he saw.

"Yes," he said, "I think it will be all right."

"Of course it will be all right," the sallow-faced man said with a touch of asperity. He turned to Kohler. "Come with me."

They left Carl with the other man, climbed a flight of stairs and went into a small bedroom in which there was a single-bed.

"You will sleep here tonight," the sallow-faced man said. "Now, of course, you would like to take a bath." He opened a wardrobe and took out a dressing-gown and a pair of carpet slippers. "You may undress in here. Meanwhile I will go and run the bath." He draped the dressing-gown across the bottom of the bed, dropped the slippers on the floor and went out of the room without waiting for any questions or argument.

Kohler felt in no need of a bath, but the sallow-faced man appeared to have been giving an order rather than making a suggestion, so he undressed quickly, donned the dressing-gown and slippers, and left the bedroom. The bathroom was just across the landing and he could hear the water running. The sallow-faced man met him in the doorway.

"Take care," he said. "The water is very hot. Take as long as you like; there is no hurry."

Kohler said nothing. He went into the bathroom and closed the door. He had a leisurely bath, and when he returned to the bedroom he found that all the discarded clothing, as well as his wallet and ship's pass, had disappeared. On the bed were a pair of dark grey trousers, a Harris tweed jacket and a fawn, single-breasted raincoat, together with a set of clean underclothing. On the floor was a pair of brown suede shoes.

He took off the dressing-gown and began to dress; and he was pleased to discover that the clothes were a rather better fit and quality than those he had discarded. What was more, they were all brand new.

There was something in the breast pocket of the jacket. He put his hand in and pulled out a leather wallet containing one hundred pounds in notes of various denominations. With the wallet was a West German passport made out in the name of Kurt Muller. The photograph inside was of himself.

*

Kohler left Ipswich soon after breakfast. He had had a good night's sleep and was feeling in rather better spirits. The sallow-faced man, the man named Carl and the man who was about Kohler's size shared breakfast with him, but it was a silent meal, no one appearing to have any desire for conversation. The only information Kohler gleaned was that he would be going to London and that Carl would drive him there in the Allegro. As well as the clothes he was wearing he had been provided with two spare sets of underclothing, two pairs of pyjamas, an electric razor and other toilet gear and a suitcase in which to carry the things.

He asked Carl why he was being sent to London, but the answer he got was not very satisfactory.

"Because that is where you are going to live."

"As Kurt Muller?"

"As Kurt Muller."

"For what purpose?"

"That is not for me to tell you. I am just the driver. I suppose someone will give you instructions in due course."

Kohler thought it probable. It was hardly likely that he had been sent to England merely to get him away from Germany, or even to act as a counter in some strange game of interchanging identities. Thinking of that prompted him to ask another question.

"Who was the other man?"

"What other man?" Carl asked.

"The younger one. Not the one who was giving the orders."

Carl glanced at him with an odd kind of smile on his pale, broad face. "Didn't you recognise him?"

"No. Should I have?"

"I thought you might have done. That was Jan Rakowski, a steward on board the Polish cargo ship 'Josef Pulaski'."

"He spoke excellent English. One might almost have taken him for an Englishman."

"Yes," Carl said, again with that odd smile twisting his mouth, "one might, mightn't one?"

*

By mid-morning they were in London. Carl seemed to be familiar with the way and handled the Allegro in the traffic of the capital as though he had had plenty of practice in that particular line.

"You seem to know your way around," Kohler said. "No doubt you have been here before."

"No doubt," Carl said, but he did not amplify the answer.

Kohler had never previously been in London and was completely lost, but they arrived eventually at a rather shabby old house in a narrow street and Carl informed him that this was where he would be taking up residence in a bed-sitting room that had already been taken for him in the name of Kurt Muller.

The room was on the first floor, and they were taken up to it by a bleak, skinny woman wearing a shapeless cardigan and a black skirt. Her name was Mrs Wilton and she was the landlady who occupied a small flat on the ground floor. She informed Kohler that the rent for his room had been paid for two weeks in advance, but that after that she would expect him to pay for it on a weekly basis.

"It's a nice room," she said. "It's one of the nicest in the 'ouse." She spoke with a wheezing sound, as though she suffered from asthma. She had a long, mournful face and greying blonde hair that looked as though it had been trimmed with a pair of garden shears. "You'll be comfortable, I'm sure."

When Kohler saw the room it occurred to him that if this was one of the nicest in the house the standard could not be very high. The furniture looked as if it had been picked up secondhand and had not been of very good quality even when new; there was a piece of worn carpet on the floor and some faded paper on the walls; an old iron grate was half hidden by a gas-fire standing in the hearth, but it was not alight and the air was distinctly chilly.

Mrs Wilton said: "You're foreign, aren't you, Mr Muller?" She pronounced the name as though it rhymed with "duller".

"I am German," Kohler said.

Mrs Wilton sniffed. "Well, I'm not prejudiced. Take as you find, I always say. The bathroom is at the end of the passage. Leave it as you would wish to find it, if you don't mind."

She shuffled away and they could hear her going down

the stairs. Carl turned the tap on the gas-fire and lit it with a match.

"You'll need to keep some change to feed the meter," he said. "And I advise you to buy a street map of London."

"I will do that," Kohler said.

"I'll leave you now. I've done my job. I expect they'll get in touch with you very soon." He did not say who "they" were.

In fact the contact was made that afternoon. Kohler had been out to get a meal, but he had not gone far. He had eaten in a rather grubby little café and had returned within an hour. Mrs Wilton appeared in the hallway when he went in and stopped him as he was about to climb the stairs.

"Oh, Mr Muller," she said, "there's a gentleman come to see you. Said 'e was a friend, so I took the liberty of letting 'im into your room. I 'ope it's all right."

"Yes," Kohler said. "I was expecting someone."

The man had lighted the gas-fire and was sitting in the better of the two armchairs. He was a small man, immaculately dressed in a dark blue pin-striped suit, and his coat, hat, gloves and rolled umbrella were lying in a neat array on the divan-bed.

"Ah, Muller," he said; "so you have returned." He glanced at his wrist-watch. "I have been waiting fifteen minutes." He spoke with a trace of acidity, as though reprimanding Kohler for causing him to waste very valuable time. "Close the door."

Kohler did so. "I am sorry. I went out to get some food. I did not know when you would come."

"Very well, very well," the man said. He looked closely at Kohler. "So you are the one they have sent us." His tone might have been taken to imply that he was not entirely pleased; that Kohler did not impress him at all favourably. His face, Kohler thought, was like a plastic mask; there was a leaden, almost corpse-like look about it that was strangely repellent; the nose was narrow, pinched in just above the nostrils, lips thin, opening no more than a fraction of an inch when he spoke, eyes cold as a snake's, hair covering his head thinly like a close-fitting skull-cap of black crape. "Do you," he asked "consider yourself to be a competent agent?"

"I do my best," Kohler said.

The black-haired man made a slight grimace. "That is not an answer to my question. However, we will pass over that. Your opinion of yourself is of little importance; you have been sent and we must make use of you. No doubt you wish to know who I am. For the purpose of the exercise my name is Lorenz. It is from me that you will take your orders. Is that clear?"

"Quite clear," Kohler said. "But what is the exercise?"

For answer Lorenz took a small photograph from his pocket and handed it to Kohler. It was the portrait of a fair-haired, bearded man whose age was difficult to judge; there were deep creases round his eyes and he could have been in his middle forties, though he might well have been younger. Kohler studied the photograph, then looked at Lorenz, waiting for further information.

"That," Lorenz said, "is Lajos Karakas, a Hungarian defector, now working for the BBC."

"So?" Kohler said.

"So your task is to kill him."

Kohler looked unhappy. He had been forced to carry out a killing in Bonn and had not enjoyed it; now it seemed he had been sent to England to do a similar job. It was not what he had expected, and certainly not what he would have desired.

Lorenz was watching him narrowly. There was a piece of information he had received in the coded communication regarding Kohler to the effect that the man was

expendable. If Kohler had known this he might have been
even less happy than he was; but Lorenz did not tell him;
possibly he thought the knowledge might discourage him.

Besides being unhappy, Kohler was puzzled. "A
Hungarian! What is our interest in him?"

"None," Lorenz said. "It is simply a question of friendly
co-operation."

"You mean we have been asked by Hungarian Security
to eliminate Karakas for them?"

"That is, I imagine, the situation. In return for an
equivalent favour, of course. But it is not important. You
have your orders."

"But how – when?" Kohler gazed at Lorenz in genuine
bewilderment.

"As to the means," Lorenz said, "that is for you to
decide. As to when, there is no immediate hurry; you may
take as much time as you wish – within reason. As long as
we can assure our Hungarian friends that the matter has
been taken in hand ..."

Kohler looked again at the photograph. Karakas had
been smiling at the camera, and the impression one had
was of a pleasant, friendly man without a care in the world.
And he, Kohler, was to kill this man, whom he had never
seen and of whose very existence he had until a few
moments ago been utterly unaware.

"This," Lorenz said, "is his address." He had taken a
small card from his pocket, which he now passed to Kohler.
The address was in Hendon and meant nothing to Kohler.
"He works," Lorenz continued, "at Bush House, which is
the headquarters of the BBC's External Services. That is in
Aldwych."

"I know nothing of London."

"So you must learn. You are not incapable of reading a
map, I hope."

"No."

"That is no problem then. Our information is that Karakas usually arrives for work some time between half-past five and six o'clock in the evening." Lorenz stood up. "I think that is all. Have you any questions?"

"There is the matter of money," Kohler said. "I have one hundred pounds, but –"

"You will receive a remittance in cash every other week, which will be sufficient for you if you are not extravagant; you cannot expect to be maintained in luxury. The money will be sent to you by post to this address."

"And if I should need to get in touch with you?"

"That should not be necessary. In an emergency, however, call this number." He took the card from Kohler and wrote on it a telephone number. "Say that M wishes to speak to L. But I repeat that it should not be necessary. This is your job, Muller, and you must handle it in your own way without assistance; that is what you are being paid for. And incidentally, you had better memorise that address and the telephone number and then destroy the card."

He left then. Kohler smoked a cigarette and tried to decide what would be the best method of killing Lajos Karakas. Two hours later he had still come to no satisfactory conclusion.

10

THE SHIVERS

The man who had once been Hans Schmidt, then Hans
Kohler, briefly Oskar Braun and Jan Rakowski, and was
now Kurt Muller had been living in his bed-sitting room for
little more than a week when the incident occurred that was
to lead to his meeting with Angela Harka and the
consequences that followed. During the week of his
residence Muller had not been idle; he had bought a street
atlas of London and its outer suburbs and had begun to
make himself familiar with the area in which his intended
victim might be expected to move.

On the third day he travelled out to Hendon on the
Underground and located the house where Karakas was
living. It was some ten minutes walk from Hendon Central
Station, a modest terrace house in a quiet tree-lined road,
standing some five or six yards back from the pavement
behind a small front garden. Muller glanced at it in passing
but did not loiter. He walked to the end of the road and
then returned. As he was approaching the house for the
second time, the front door opened and a woman came out.
She was wearing a brown tweed coat and a headscarf and
was carrying a shopping-basket and a rolled umbrella.
Muller wondered whether she was Karakas's wife; Lorenz
had not said whether or not he was married. The woman

passed by him on the pavement but showed no interest. He tried to figure out in his mind whether, if this woman were Karakas's wife, it would complicate the operation, but came to the conclusion that it would not. He had never intended killing the man in his own house.

The following day Muller was in the crescent known as Aldwych at a little before half-past five, and he hung around within sight of the entrance to Bush House, keeping an eye open for anyone who might look like the man in the photograph that Lorenz had given him. His luck was in, for at ten minutes to six, as he was patrolling near the corner of Kingsway and Drury Lane, Karakas walked past so close that Muller could have touched him by simply holding out his hand. There could be no doubt that it was Karakas; he was bareheaded, and the resemblance to the photograph was unmistakable. He had apparently walked down Drury Lane from the direction of New Oxford Street, and he crossed the road and disappeared inside the massive structure of Bush House on the opposite side.

It gave Muller a curious feeling, this first sight of the man he had been ordered to kill; until this moment Karakas had been to him no more than a name and a face in a photograph, something vague and shadowy and undefined; now in an instant that had all been changed; now he was a creature of flesh and blood, solid and real; a living, breathing fellow human. Muller felt suddenly cold; a shudder passed through his frame; he swayed slightly, as though a gust of wind had caught him. But he took a grip on himself; this would never do; he must not make himself conspicuous. He turned and walked away.

*

The next day he was at Hendon Central Station when Karakas arrived on foot. Muller was gratified to see him; it proved that he had been correct in his supposition that Karakas did not use a car to get to work but travelled by the Underground.

When Karakas boarded the train Muller followed him into the carriage and took a seat from which he could keep the man under observation without being in the other's direct line of vision. Again as Muller had expected, Karakas left the train at Tottenham Court Road and crossed over into New Oxford Street. Muller followed at a reasonable distance and saw Karakas turn down Druty Lane.

It was obvious where he was going; nevertheless, Muller felt constrained to follow, and as he himself came into Drury Lane he saw Karakas glance back over his shoulder. It was only a momentary glance, but, although there were other people between the two of them, it seemed to him that for that one moment the man's eyes were directed straight at him. He told himself that this was sheer fancy and that there was nothing significant in it even if Karakas had glanced at him, but he could not entirely convince himself. He watched Karakas cross over to Bush House and disappear inside the building, and then he returned to his room, feeling vaguely disquieted.

*

He might have been even more disquieted if he had known just how observant Lajos Karakas was. Karakas was only too well aware that men in his position were at risk; some had in fact been killed by agents of the security services of those East European countries from which they had defected, and he had no desire to be added to that number.

So he kept himself on the alert, and he had spotted Muller at Hendon Central Station and had immediately recognised him as the man he had passed at the Aldwych end of Drury Lane the previous day.

It seemed an odd coincidence, and when Muller got into the same carriage and took a seat not far away; when he also got out at Tottenham Court Road and followed a little way behind Karakas down New Oxford Street and into Drury Lane it began to look very much like something more than mere coincidence. Karakas decided, therefore, to be even more than usual on the alert, and if necessary to take some action on his own account to guard against what he was now convinced was a possible threat to his life.

*

For his part, Muller felt it might be best to do nothing more for a few days. The weekend was coming up; he would relax and spend a bit of time exploring London and visiting some of the usual tourist attractions. After all, had not Lorenz told him that there was no need for haste in dealing with Karakas?

It was on the Monday that, returning home after an evening devoted to tasting the diversions of the West End, he was set upon by a gang of young thugs and fortuitously rescued by Angela Harka and her friends. It did not take him long to become aware of the very special interest that the fair-haired girl was taking in him, and his immediate impulse was to repulse her, seeing her as nothing more than an embarrassment. But he soon began to alter his mind. He was genuinely attracted to her; she was no Gerda Vogel, and with her he did not have to feign an interest he did not feel.

Matters progressed remarkably quickly, and within a few weeks they were living together in the furnished maisonette in Clapham. It was altogether more comfortable than the bed-sitter at Mrs Wilton's, and Muller congratulated himself on having made a very shrewd move. To explain his reason for being in England and having no regular job to go to, he told Miss Harka that he was gathering material for a book. He gave only the sketchiest of information regarding his background, but it seemed to be enough; she asked few questions and accepted him at his face value.

His chief cause for concern was the assignment that was still not carried out; it hung over him like a dark cloud. During the period since he had become involved with this girl he had done nothing more in the matter of Lajos Karakas, and time was slipping away. He had had no further contact with Lorenz, but the remittances had begun to come through; he had made a bargain with Mrs Wilton to forward them to his new address and had not thought it necessary to inform Lorenz of the alteration in his domestic arrangements. The truth was that he feared Lorenz might not altogether approve, and he wished to keep this news from the man as long as possible.

Meanwhile, he made no move to tackle the Karakas job, and with every passing day became less and less inclined to do so. He was paying nothing towards the rent of the maisonette; he had made a tentative offer of help in that way but Angela had refused to hear of any such thing.

"Kurt, darling," she said, "I've got plenty of money and there's not the least need for you to chip in."

"But I ought to pay my share. It's not right that you should carry the whole burden."

"But I want to, don't you see? It makes me happy to do things for you. Don't you want me to be happy?"

When she put it like that there seemed no way of arguing with her, and he did not try. If it pleased her, why make an issue of it? She was a charming girl and he was enjoying the easy living. If only there had not been that threatening cloud hanging over him. But perhaps if he ignored it, it would go away.

Then Lorenz stepped into the picture and he knew that

the cloud would certainly not go away. It was seven o'clock in the evening when someone rang the doorbell. Angela went to see who it was and came back to the sitting-room with Lorenz in tow, looking as neat and dapper and corpse-like as ever.

"Good evening, Muller," Lorenz said. "I went to your old lodgings and was informed that you had moved to this address." He spoke calmly, smoothly, and his leaden features were without expression; but Muller detected a glint in his eye and was afraid. He knew that Lorenz was filled with a cold, deadly anger.

"Yes," he said. "I should have told you."

"Indeed you should," Lorenz said. He turned to the girl, oozing urbanity. "One likes to know where one's friends are hiding; one doesn't wish to have to do detective work in order to find them."

She smiled at him, a little uncertainly. "I suppose not."

Lorenz was wearing his coat and was carrying his hat and rolled umbrella in his left hand. She offered to relieve him of them, but he politely refused.

"I shall not be staying long. I merely wished to have a word or two with our friend here."

He paused, looking at her. It was as much as to say that he wished to have the word in private, and she took the hint.

"I have some cooking to do. Perhaps you will excuse me."

She left the room and closed the door behind her. Muller glanced at Lorenz with some uneasiness.

"You have an explanation for all this?" Lorenz asked; a slight flutter of the hand indicating the room, everything.

Muller gave a brief account of the attack on him by thugs and the subsequent events. "It just happened."

The glint was in Lorenz's eye again. "Are you mad? That girl –"

"She knows nothing."

"I hope for your sake that she does not. You have been a fool, Muller. I was not greatly impressed with you at our first meeting, but I did not think you would be quite such a fool as this."

Muller was suddenly defensive. "I don't see that there is anything foolish in what I have done. I can operate from here as well as from that room."

"And how far, may I ask, have your operations progressed?" There was a sneer in Lorenz's voice. "What have you done so far?"

"I have been feeling the ground. I have observed Karakas's movements. I know his habits."

"It should hardly have taken you so long to do that."

"You told me there was no hurry."

"As I remember it, I said you might take as much time as you wished, within reason. But now perhaps we should ask ourselves when further delay begins to be unreasonable. I suggest to you, Muller, that you should devote some careful thought to this question, and that you should see whether it is not possible to accelerate things. Do I make myself clear?"

He was making himself very clear indeed: what he was saying was that Muller had delayed long enough and had better get on with the job. He lifted his umbrella and touched Muller lightly on the chest with the point of it. Muller could feel the coldness of the ferule striking through the thin material of his shirt and chilling a small circle of skin. He wondered uneasily whether this might not perhaps be one of those cunningly constructed umbrellas which at the touch of a button could shoot a poisoned dart into a man or thrust out a steel blade like the tip of a rapier. He was rather relieved when Lorenz lowered the umbrella without doing anything lethal with it.

"Well," he said, "it is time for me to go. I trust you will

bear in mind what I have said. You have done one very
foolish thing, Muller; do not compound the error by doing
another. We should not wish to have our trust in you
confounded; nor should we wish to be forced to take
punitive measures."

Muller knew that he was being warned, and when he
closed the front door on the departing Lorenz he was far
less happy than he had been before the man's arrival.

"Who was he?" Angela asked, coming in from the
kitchen. "Is he really a friend of yours?"

"I am not sure I would call him that," Muller said.

"I didn't like him. I felt there was something evil about
him. He gave me the shivers."

"To tell you the truth," Muller said, "he gives me the
shivers too."

*

The day after Lorenz's visit Muller again travelled from
Hendon Central to Tottenham Court Road in the same
Underground Railway carriage as Lajos Karakas. He
wished to make sure that Karakas had made no alteration
to his usual routine. Karakas gave no sign of having noticed
him, and he came to the conclusion that he had probably
been mistaken on the previous occasion in supposing that
he had been spotted. On that point, however, he was quite
wrong. Karakas had in fact been on the lookout for Muller
ever since then, and not having seen him for a few weeks
had begun to think he might have been mistaken in
suspecting Muller of ill intentions towards him. Now,
however, all his earlier suspicions were revived, and he
knew what he had to do.

*

The next day Muller was once again in the same carriage
as Karakas on his journey to work, but this time Muller was

carrying a small canvas holdall. There was nothing in the holdall but a long-bladed, sharp-pointed sheath-knife, which he had bought at a shop in the Strand. It was his intention when they left the train at Tottenham Court Road to get close to Karakas in the crush, put his hand into the holdall and thrust the knife through the canvas and into Karakas's heart. No one would be aware of what had happened and he would be able to get away in the crowd without fear of detection.

It did not work out, however; for when the train arrived at Tottenham Court Road Station there were so many people between him and Karakas, all waiting for the doors to open, that it was quite impossible to get near the man. To attempt to elbow his way through such a tightly-packed human barrier would have inevitably attracted unwanted attention to himself. He accepted the situation and allowed Karakas to go.

*

A fair-haired man wearing a short sheepskin coat and a green check cap had been sitting next to Karakas all the way from Hendon, but the two had not spoken to each other, and Muller had taken little notice of the man. When Karakas got up from his seat and made his way to the doors as the train approached Tottenham Court Road the man in the sheepskin coat remained where he was, and it was not until the crush had built up in the doorway that he made a move. He was thus behind Muller, and when Muller left the train he was unaware that he himself was being followed.

He was unaware also that the man's name was Grigor Stanev, that he was of Bulgarian origin and that he was a member of a small group of Eastern European emigrants calling itself the Exiles Mutual Protection Association, or EMPA for short. This group had come together when it

had become apparent that the lives of defectors from
communist countries were in danger and that the police
could not be entirely relied upon for protection. Karakas
was a member of EMPA, and when he became convinced
that Muller was keeping him under observation he reported
the fact and requested that something might be done about
it. The result was that Stanev had been deputed to carry
out a piece of investigation. It was for this reason that he
was on the train with Karakas, and for this reason also that
when Muller came out of Tottenham Court Road Station
Stanev was on his tail.

It was so far from Muller's mind that anyone might be
following him that Stanev's task was made perfectly simple.
When Muller arrived back at the maisonette near Clapham
Common Stanev was still not far behind. He saw Muller let
himself into the house and close the door. Muller had never
once looked back.

11

SPIDER'S PARLOUR

"What did you think of Angela?" Miss Donson asked. She
and Grant had stayed an hour at the maisonette, and then
Grant had driven her back to the flat. "Did you like her?"

"I saw nothing about her to dislike," Grant said. "She
may not be very wise perhaps –"

"You're referring to Kurt, of course. You didn't like
him?"

"I wouldn't say that exactly. It's more a question of not
entirely trusting him."

"And why don't you trust him?"

"Well, for a start I tend to be rather a suspicious person
by nature. Occupational disease, you might call it."

"The private eye syndrome?"

Grant smiled. "That's about it."

"And is that all the reason you have for not trusting
him?"

"Not quite. There's this story of his about being in
England to gather material for a book."

"It sounds possible to me."

"Maybe it is; but when I asked him some questions
about it he started off by being pretty evasive, and then
clammed up altogether. Frankly, he doesn't strike me as
being a writer."

"So you can recognise a writer simply by looking at him?"

"No, but one gets an impression. My impression of friend Muller is that he's hiding something."

"Such as?"

"I don't know. But I do know he's a bit edgy. All the time we were there he was like a cat on hot bricks. Didn't you notice?"

"He may have been rather nervous. It doesn't prove anything though, does it?"

"That's true. All the same –"

"What you're saying is that you don't think he's the kind of person Miss Rogerson would approve of as an intimate companion for her niece?"

"I'm dead certain of that."

"Are you going to tell her?"

"Not immediately. I'll try to find out a bit more about him first."

"Do you still want my help?"

"If you can spare the time I'd be very grateful for any help you can give."

"Oh," she said, "now that I'm out of a job I've got all the time in the world. Are you going to stay for supper?"

"Is that an invitation?"

She gave him a charming smile. "I'm having pity on you. You don't really want to go back to that grubby little flat of yours yet, do you?"

"No," he said; "now that you come to mention it, I don't."

*

"Who is this man, Grant?" Muller said. "Where did Carol pick him up?"

"You know as much about him as I do," Angela said. "I'd never seen him before I opened the door and found him standing on the doorstep. But you heard what she said; he's a representative for a double-glazing firm."

"Where would she have met a window salesman?"

"Perhaps he knocked on her door and tried to interest her in some double-glazing."

"I do not believe it. I think he is something else."

"Now why on earth should he be something else? Why shouldn't he be what he says he is? Kurt, darling, what's the matter? You almost make me think you're afraid of this man."

Muller turned on her. "Afraid! Why do you say that? Why should I be afraid?"

"There!" she said. "Now you really are being touchy. What's bothering you?"

Muller made an effort to control himself; it was unwise to behave like this. But the fact was that he was indeed on edge, and had been so ever since boarding the Tube train at Hendon Central. Throughout the journey he had been steeling himself to carry out the killing, and then, when it had been impossible to do so, he had felt exhausted by the mental strain.

He had returned straight home and had been there little more than an hour when Carol Donson had turned up with a complete stranger named Sam Grant. And Grant had proceeded to ask questions, as though he had come there with the express purpose of probing into his, Muller's, background. Why had he been so inquisitive? And who in hell was he?

"Nothing's bothering me," he said. "I'm just a little tired, that's all."

"I expect you've done too much walking round London; it does wear people out. Why don't you let me come with you next time? It might be a help to have someone who knows the way around."

Muller firmly rejected the idea. "I can find my own way

around; there is no need for you to bother."

"But it would be no bother; I'd like to do it."

"No; I must be on my own. It is the only way I can concentrate on my work." He could see that she was disappointed, and perhaps only partly convinced by the reason he had given. He tried to make it more plausible. "Don't think I am not grateful for the offer; but having you with me would be a distraction – a very lovely distraction of course, but not really a help with what I am doing."

She made a slight grimace. "You've never told me much about that, have you?"

"It would not interest you. It is just a matter of taking notes."

"You wouldn't like to let me read them?"

"Can you read German?"

"No."

"Then I am afraid you would not get much from them."

She came and kissed him. "I love you, Kurt; you know that, don't you?"

"I hope it is so," he said.

"My darling, you can be sure it is. But sometimes I think you like to make a big mystery of yourself. Is there something you have to hide from me? Have you some dark secret that must not be revealed?"

She spoke jokingly and he answered in the same tone: "Of course. But not just one, many. And I will never tell you them because I am sure it is the mystery that attracts you to me. Get rid of the mystery and what do I become? Just an ordinary uninteresting man."

"You could never be uninteresting to me, Kurt."

"Nor you to me," he said. "Nor you to me."

Later he again raised the subject of Sam Grant, as though he could not keep away from it. "I feel sure that man is not what he said he was. I should like to know what he really does for a living."

"Why does it interest you so much?"

"I have an insatiable curiosity about people I meet; didn't you realise that? And I should like to know whether I am right in my suspicion."

"Well," she said, "if you're really so keen to find out about him, I could ask Carol. I'm sure she would tell me the truth."

"Yes," Muller said; "please do that."

"But the answer will probably be that he's just a double-glazing salesman."

"Well, we shall see."

*

"He is German," Stanev said. "His name is Muller and he is living with a woman named Harka, who is English."

Stanev was reporting to a handful of men sitting round a table in a public-house in a narrow street leading off the Strand. There were five of them altogether, and they were all members of EMPA. Karakas was one of the group; he had taken a break from his work at Bush House and had joined the others to hear Stanev's account of his tailing of the man with the canvas holdall.

Stanev had been lucky; after observing Muller let himself into the maisonette he had found a neighbour who was perfectly willing, even eager, to talk about Muller and Miss Harka. This neighbour was a woman, a Mrs Andrews, widowed, living by herself and with time on her hands. Stanev rang her doorbell and was ready with a story about being employed by a hire-purchase firm to make discreet inquiries concerning the credit-worthiness of would-be customers. His name was Smith and he would, he said, be most obliged if Mrs Andrews would help him – in the strictest confidence, naturally.

He need hardly have bothered with the story: Mrs Andrews almost dragged him inside and ushered him into a small, overheated, over-furnished sitting-room. Within two minutes he found himself ensconced in an armchair with a glass of ruby port in his hand and Mrs Andrews sitting scarcely three feet away from him with a glass of the same liquid in her own much-beringed fingers.

"I don't usually indulge at this time of an evening, Mr Smith, but just to be sociable ..." She was a plump, red-haired woman of about forty, with a voluptuous look about her.

Stanev felt rather like a fly that had walked into the spider's parlour. Mrs Andrews seemed ready, figuratively speaking, to gobble him up with tremendous relish. But she had the information he wanted; she was obviously an inquisitive, prying sort of person with time to ask questions and observe movements from her lace-curtained windows, and she had made it her business to find out all she could regarding the new occupants of the house next door.

"They're not married, you know. He's older than she is, and I happen to know she's the one that pays the rent. It wouldn't surprise me if he was some kind of gigolo and she was keeping him, not a bit, it wouldn't. These foreigners, they're not like you and me, are they, Mr Smith?"

"No," Stanev said, "I suppose they're not."

She leaned towards him and rested a hand on his knee, her heavy breasts hanging like two large melons precariously supported by the thin fabric of her dress. "If you ask me, that's a man as'd bear watching. Got no regular job, you know; comes and goes any old time. What's he up to? Nothing legal, I'll be bound."

"So you think he's a criminal?"

"I'm not saying that." Mrs Andrews took the hand off Stanev's knee and sat back in her chair. "But there's funny things goes on these days and you never know where you are." She gave him a very knowing look and sipped her port, holding the stem of the glass delicately between thumb and forefinger.

Stanev saw that he had reached the limit of her knowledge regarding Kurt Muller and that he was likely to get nothing more from her but speculation. He could do his own work in that line, so he finished his drink, stood the glass on a table beside the chair and got to his feet.

"You've been very helpful, Mrs Andrews, and I'm much obliged. Now I must go."

"Must you really? Do have another glass of port first. One for the road, as the saying is."

"Thank you," Stanev said, "but no. You mustn't try to make me tipsy."

She simpered. It was rather grotesque in one of her age, an attempt at girlishness which did not go with the face or the figure. She came to the door with him, and the hallway was so narrow that he could only just squeeze past her as she held the doorknob; he could feel those heavy, melon-like breasts squashing him against the wall as though reluctant to let him go; but with a desperate effort he made his escape.

"Come again," Mrs Andrews said. "Any time you're passing, just pop in."

"I'll do that," Stanev said; but he had no intention of ever seeing her again. Another time he might not escape; the spider might really gobble him up.

*

The group listened to his report in silence. When he had finished Karakas said:

"So his name is Muller and he has no job. It confirms my suspicions."

A small dark man named Puskis expressed some doubt. "Why would a German wish to kill you? A Hungarian, yes; but a German –"

"How do we know he is not a Hungarian posing as a German? That is possible."

"It is possible," Staney said. "It is also possible that he is an East German agent co-operating with Hungarian Security. Either way, he could be dangerous. I think we should take measures."

"Without being certain?" Puskis said. "We must be sure about him first."

"If we wait to be sure it could be too late."

"That is true. But to take action without being completely certain might be to eliminate an innocent man."

"That is a risk we have to take."

"I do not agree," Puskis said. "I say that it is a risk we must not take."

The other two men joined in the discussion, and they argued the matter out, keeping their voices low so that no one who was not sitting at the table could hear them above the general buzz of conversation. When the meeting broke up they had still not come to a decision.

*

"He's here to gather material for a book," Grant said. "He's thirty to thirty-five, I'd say; fair-haired, lean, not particularly handsome but with a certain charm; the kind of man a woman would probably find it easy to fall in love with."

"Um!" Mr Peking said. "So you think Miss Harka is in love with him?"

"I've no doubt about it. Whether he's in love with her or is simply making use of her is another question."

"Making use of her in what way?"

"For free meals and accommodation. It looks like a pretty cushy number for him."

Mr Peking looked perturbed; he was possibly reflecting

that it was not the kind of thing he wished to report to Miss Rogerson. "And he's a writer, you say?"

"That's what he says he is."

Mr Peking leaned back in his chair and cast a searching look at Grant across the meticulously tidy expanse of his desk. "Do I detect a note of scepticism in that remark?"

"Possibly."

"So you think he is not telling the truth?"

"It wouldn't surprise me."

"Why would he tell a lie about it?"

"I've no idea."

Mr Peking leaned forward and drummed on the desk with his well-manicured fingers. "This doesn't sound at all healthy. It has a most disagreeable odour. Wouldn't you agree?"

"Oh, I don't know," Grant said. "Even if the man isn't a writer he may be quite above board."

"There seems to be very good reason for having some doubt about that."

"Well, there's nothing more we can do. I suppose you will want me to get on to a different case now."

"Certainly not," Peking said. "Do you imagine I can leave matters like this? What do you suppose Miss Rogerson would say? No, Grant; for the present you will remain on this case and no other."

"Doing what exactly?"

"Doing what! Finding out more about this damned German, of course. And incidentally keeping an eye on Miss Harka."

Grant shrugged. "Well, if you say so."

*

Angela Harka paid a call on Carol Donson in the afternoon of the day after Miss Donson had brought Sam

Grant to meet her. Muller had gone out, presumably to gather more material for his book. He had been carrying the small canvas holdall which he had taken with him the previous day, explaining that he might possibly buy a few things and that it would be useful for carrying them if he did.

"I wondered whether I would find you in," she said. "No new job yet?"

"No. It's deadly boring. I'm glad you dropped in. One gets tired of one's own company. Let's have some tea and a good talk. You're not in a hurry?"

"No. Kurt has gone out, so I'm absolutely free for a few hours."

Later, over the teacups, she brought up the interesting subject of Sam Grant. "So the new boy-friend isn't around today?"

"Boy-friend?"

"Mr Grant."

"Oh, him!" Miss Donson gave a laugh. "I'd hardly call him a boy-friend. Just an acquaintance."

"Really?"

"Yes, really."

"Maybe it'll grow into more than that. Let's hope so. He seems nice."

"You think so?"

"Don't you?"

"Perhaps he is."

"You don't sound very sure about it. How did you come to meet him? Did he try to sell you a window?"

"A window?" Miss Donson looked puzzled.

"It's what he does for a living, isn't it? Double-glazing, you know."

"Oh, yes. Yes, of course."

Miss Harka drank some more tea and smiled knowingly. "It isn't true, is it?"

"Not true! Now what makes you think that?"

"The way you said it. You can't fool me. Now come clean. Why not admit it?"

Miss Donson hesitated a moment, then admitted it. "All right; so he doesn't sell double-glazing."

"What does he do?"

This time Miss Donson hesitated rather longer before answering; but finally she said: "Well, I don't see that there's any harm in telling you. He's an inquiry agent."

Miss Harka stared at her. "You mean a private eye?"

"I don't think that's what he calls himself; but yes, he is. He works for a firm called the Peking Inquiry Agency."

"You mean to say he's come all the way from China?"

"No; it's a London firm. The head of it is a man named Peking."

"How tremendously exciting. I've never met a real live private eye before. You must bring him round again so I can have a second look."

"I'm not sure I'll be seeing him again."

"But of course you will. What's he inquiring about? I mean why did he call on you? You haven't done anything illegal, have you?"

"Of course not. It was a mistake really. I think he was looking for somebody else."

"But you don't know who?"

"No," Miss Donson said, without batting an eyelid, "I don't know who."

12

NO MORE DOUBTS

Muller was still unaware that Karakas had any suspicions regarding him when he travelled out to Hendon for the second successive day with the knife concealed in the holdall. He had no reason to suppose that Karakas had spotted him as a possible threat to his life, for the Hungarian defector was on the platform at the usual time waiting for the train to take him to work, and he gave no sign of recognising Muller.

When the train arrived Muller followed Karakas into the carriage and took a seat somewhat closer to him than on the previous day. He felt his nervousness increasing as the train rattled on its way, and when it went underground and the sides of the tunnel closed in he had a sense of being trapped. He experienced a feeling of claustrophobia, and he began to sweat under the armpits, and his hands were moist in the palms.

He read the names of the stations as they came to them: Belsize Park, Chalk Farm, Camden Town – each one represented another step nearer the fatal moment, nearer the deadly act he had to perform. It occurred to him suddenly that he might yet postpone it; he could even leave the train at one of the stations still lying between him and

Tottenham Court Road. Nevertheless, he remained seated.
When people began to get out at Euston he half rose from
his seat; but he sat down again. In quick succession the
platforms of Warren Street and Goodge Street came into
view, remained there a few seconds as the doors opened and
closed, and then slid away behind the accelerating train.
Now he was on the last lap of his journey and the next stop
would be Tottenham Court Road. There was a kind of
inevitability about it now. It had to happen.

He was breathing rapidly, as though he had been
engaged in some violent exercise rather than sitting
motionless in the carriage. He was aware of the thumping
of his heart; his mouth felt dry; and there was a slight
drumming in his head. He wondered whether he was going
to faint.

The train began to slow down. He saw Karakas stand up
and move towards the doors, and as if suddenly galvanised
into action he himself got up from his seat and moved
quickly to place himself immediately behind the man. He
had the canvas holdall gripped in his left hand and was
holding it in front of him. With his right hand he drew back
the zipper, slipped his hand into the bag and grasped the
handle of the knife.

The train had reached the station and was coming to a
halt. Muller was pushed forward by a crush of passengers
behind him and was forced into contact with Karakas.
Karakas turned his head and seemed to become aware for
the first time that Muller was so close to him. Their glances
met, and Muller could read the sudden apprehension in
Karakas's eyes. He realised then that Karakas knew what
he intended to do.

Again Muller had a thought of calling it off; even now it
was not too late. But then the train came to a halt and the
doors started to open and he thought of Lorenz. He

tightened his grip on the knife and made a lunge with it through the canvas of the holdall.

But he had hesitated a moment too long; Karakas moved in the very instant of the attack and ruined Muller's aim. Instead of sinking deeply into Karakas's back and penetrating to some vital part of his body, the knife merely ripped his coat on the left-hand side and did no more than lightly scratch the flesh.

Muller, carried forward by the sheer force of his thrust, stumbled out of the carriage as the doors came open, still gripping the holdall with his left hand and the knife with his right. He heard Karakas give a sharp cry of pain, or it might have been shock, but he did not look back. He recovered his balance almost immediately, drew the knife back into the holdall, removed his right hand and refastened the zipper. He walked rapidly, resisting the impulse to run, and was soon just one of the crowd hurrying towards the escalators. It was doubtful whether anyone but himself and Karakas realised what had happened.

*

"You did what?" Grant said, staring at Carol Donson, who stared coolly back at him – as she had every right to do, being in her own flat.

"I told her you were a private eye," she said. "She didn't believe that rubbish about double-glazing. She didn't think you had the look of a glazier – even a single one."

"And so you told her the truth?"

"Yes. There wasn't any harm in it, was there?"

"But I told you my instructions were to make discreet inquiries. Now you've let the cat out of the bag and Miss Harka will know what I'm doing."

"Why should she? I didn't tell her you were investigating

her, and I don't think it even crossed her mind that you might be. The fact is she seemed quite thrilled when I told her what you were, and she asked me to take you round there again so that she could have another look. She seems to have very romantic notions regarding private eyes.''

"But you don't?"

"I can take them or leave them," Miss Donson said.

Grant laughed. It was the first time that day he had felt much like laughing; his efforts to glean some information on the subject of Kurt Muller had not been outstandingly successful and he was feeling somewhat frustrated. He had tried the West German Embassy in Rutland Gate, but they seemed to know nothing of the Kurt Muller about whom he was inquiring. It seemed rather odd, so he tried the rival establishment in Belgrave Square, but with no better result, though the East Germans showed rather more interest and even a hint of suspicion.

He began to think he might well have been right in suspecting Muller to be not quite what he claimed to be, and he wondered whether Muller was in fact his right name and whether it might not be a good idea to get in touch with the Immigration Department or even Special Branch. But by that time it was rather late in the day and he decided to leave it for the present. Peking was not pressing him to get the business sewn up, so there seemed to be no particular urgency and no need to wear himself out in the pursuit of his duties.

He thought of returning to his flat, but the mental picture which came into his head of that somewhat unappetising abode held no great attraction for him and he decided that perhaps another call on the delectable Miss Donson, though not likely to yield anything further in the way of information regarding Kurt Muller, might nevertheless not be a complete waste of time. So to Miss Donson's he went, and was lucky enough to find the lady at home and not apparently altogether unhappy to see him.

"What have you been doing all day?" she asked.

"Oh, going hither and thither. And getting precisely nowhere."

"Sounds madly exciting."

"A typical day in the life of Samuel Grant. And what have you been doing?"

"Taking a jaundiced look at my prospects. Nothing but gloom and misery in view."

"As bad as that?"

"I think I shall have to clear out of this flat at the end of the month."

"Have you anywhere to go?"

"Nothing in sight. I'll have to start looking for a bed-sitter, I suppose." She sounded as though she were not looking forward to the search with any wild enthusiasm.

"It'll be a bit of a comedown after this."

"Well, that's the way it is."

"I've got an alternative suggestion."

"Tell me." She gave him a steady, wide-eyed look, waiting for the suggestion and maybe, he thought, guessing what it might be.

"You could move in with me."

"Well, now," she said, "that is something to think about, isn't it? Are you taking pity on me?"

Grant shook his head. "I'd say it was the other way round."

She walked over to his chair and sat down on the arm and leaned over and kissed him. She smelled very nice; and there was a lot else that was nice about her; and he could think of all sorts of reasons why it would be fun to have her moving out of this flat and into his, even if his was not quite in the same class.

"It's something to think about," she said again – musingly, as though conjuring up some kind of picture in her mind and taking a long, cool look at it. "Yes, it really is something to think about."

*

Muller found Lorenz in the Duveen Gallery at the British Museum studying the Elgin Marbles. It was the morning after the unsuccessful attempt on the life of Lajos Karakas, and Muller approached the other man with some trepidation, for he had a feeling that the interview might be a somewhat acrimonious one.

Lorenz gave no indication of having noticed his approach, but when Muller was within some three feet of him he said, without turning his head:

"So you bungled it."

Muller wondered how Lorenz knew. Was he omniscient or were they keeping watch on him? There had, as far as Muller could determine, been no report of the incident in the papers or on the broadcast news bulletins. Karakas had apparently felt no desire to publicise the fact that he had been attacked. So how did Lorenz know?

"It was bad luck," he mumbled. "He moved at the last moment."

"A competent agent makes his own luck." Lorenz's tone was acid. "Now of course the man knows you and will be on the alert. Therefore, your task will be that much more difficult."

"It may be too difficult. I am not sure I can do it now."

"You are surely not asking to be relieved of the assignment?"

"Yes," Muller said, "that is what I am asking."

"It is out of the question. The assignment has been given to you, and you will carry it out. One failure is no reason for abandoning the task."

Muller tugged nervously at his right ear and gazed at the

amazing sculptures which the Seventh Earl of Elgin had
caused to be transported from Athens to London at a cost of
seventy-five thousand pounds; but he was not really seeing
them.

"There is another reason. I am being watched."

"Watched!" Lorenz's thin eyebrows lifted slightly. "By
whom?"

"A private detective. He came to the house in Clapham
with a friend of Miss Harka's, passing himself off as a
window salesman. I had my suspicions, and yesterday
evening they were confirmed by Miss Harka. The man is an
inquiry agent and his name is –"

"Grant," Lorenz said.

Again Muller was astounded by Lorenz's apparent
ominiscience. Knowing as he did nothing of Grant's
inquiries at the East German Embassy regarding a certain
Kurt Muller, he could see no way in which Lorenz could
have obtained his information.

"You knew?"

Lorenz did not bother to answer the question. He said:
"This man must be eliminated. He is making a nuisance of
himself."

"Who will eliminate him?"

"Why," Lorenz said, "you will, of course."

Muller's heart sank; it was bad enough having to dispose
of Karakas, especially after the failure of the previous day,
but to have to deal with Grant in addition was an extra
burden, an extra problem, which he did not feel capable of
handling. Yet he had only to glance at Lorenz's grey,
expressionless face to realise that he had no choice in the
matter: he had been given an order, and again it was a
lethal order. However, he made one more appeal.

"I shall need help. This is too much for me to handle
without assistance."

Rather to his surprise, instead of brushing aside the

appeal, Lorenz, after a brief pause for consideration, said: "Very well, you shall have assistance. But only in dealing with this man, Grant. When he has been removed you must carry out the other task yourself."

Muller felt relieved. At least he would not now be entirely on his own; he would have help in putting Grant out of the way, and when that job was done perhaps the other would not seem so difficult.

"Thank you," he said. "I will do my best."

Lorenz looked at him, steely-eyed. "One can only hope, Muller, that your best may be good enough."

He did not sound as though he had any great faith that it would.

*

"So," Mr Peking said, "this fellow, Muller, appears to be something of a mystery man."

"Yes," Grant said.

"And you think he may be up to a bit of no good?"

"It seems possible."

"Any ideas regarding what?"

"Not really. It could, of course, simply be that he's found himself a nice cosy little nest and intends to make the most of his good fortune."

"That would hardly explain what he was doing in this country in the first place."

"No," Grant admitted, "it wouldn't. He certainly didn't come here with the intention of shacking up with Miss Harka; it was an accident meeting her; but he was quick to profit by it."

"Obviously an opportunist. A con man, do you think?"

"It's a possibility. Not very likely, though, I'd say. Do you want me to try Immigration or Special Branch? If he is an illegal immigrant they might be interested to hear about him."

Mr Peking stroked his beard while he gave the question some thought. Then he said: "No. I'd like if possible to keep officialdom out of this. Miss Rogerson would be most displeased if her niece were to be involved in anything sordid. We must do our best to avoid that."

"It may not be possible to avoid it."

"Well, let's not anticipate the worst. Perhaps we can frighten the man off."

"How?"

"Your very presence may do the trick. You say he now knows you're a private inquiry agent?"

"Miss Harka knows and I imagine she will have told him."

"Exactly. And if he has anything illegal to hide he'll be bound to jump to the conclusion that he's the one you're investigating. What I suggest is that you keep up the pressure; get this Miss – ah – Donson to take you round again; ask questions; lean on him a bit. He may decide things are getting too hot for comfort and decide to clear out."

Grant thought it was doubtful whether it would work, but if it was what Mr Peking wanted him to do he would give it a try. And the prospect of some more of Miss Donson's agreeable company was not at all distasteful.

"All right then," he said. "I'll lean on him a bit."

*

When Karakas gave an account of what had happened on the Tube train no member of the Exiles Mutual Protection Association could have any further doubt regarding Muller's intentions. Even Puskis had to admit that his purpose must be to kill Karakas.

"He almost did kill me," Karakas said. "If I had not moved just in time I might not have been talking to you now. As it is, I have a slight cut in the left side."

"What weapon did he use?" Stanev asked.

"I think it was a knife concealed in a small holdall."

"You have not been to the police?"

"No," Karakas said. "I think this is something we should handle ourselves. Why else did we form this group? The police have not been very effective in the past."

Stanev agreed. "We have to see to our own protection."

It was Puskis again who was not in wholehearted agreement. "In this case, however, since we know the man who made the attack, would it not be best to denounce him and let the legal authorities deal with him?"

But he was a minority of one in the group, which was assembled at its usual meeting-place, the public-house in the narrow street near the Strand. It was an old-fashioned establishment, with a lot of mahogany and zinc and mirror glass, and no one ever took any particular notice of the handful of men from Eastern Europe who made a habit of gathering there.

A heavy black-haired man with a purplish complexion and eyebrows like miniature flue-brushes, whose name was Tomic and who had been born in Yugoslavia, said: "As I see it, the duty of this group is to look to the safety of its members without recourse to outside help. For my part, I say that this bastard, Muller, should be dealt with by us. If anyone lacks the courage to take what action is necessary, then he should not be a member of the group, and the sooner he leaves it, the better." He stared fiercely at Puskis, his black eyes seeming about to take fire under the shaggy brows.

Puskis shrugged, refusing to take offence at this obvious attack upon himself. "Calm yourself. I merely suggested an alternative. But if it is the view of the majority that we should settle this matter in our own way, then of course I withdraw my suggestion."

"That is settled then," Stanev said. "Now it only remains to decide who will carry out the task. I suggest two of us should do it."

"Three," Tomic said. "To be sure."

There was a murmur of assent. Stanev nodded.

"I and two others," Karakas said.

"No," Stanev said. "He knows you. It would be unwise."

Again the murmur signified that this was agreed. Karakas accepted the decision. Stanev took a notebook from his pocket, tore out two pages, divided them into little squares of paper, marked three with crosses, folded the squares and dropped them into a hat.

"Now draw."

They drew. Tomic drew one of the marked papers; Puskis drew another; Stanev himself drew the third.

"It is settled," he said.

13

MR JACKSON

"Why do you want to go there?" Miss Donson asked.

Grant smiled. "You said your friend Angela wanted to see me again. I'd hate to disappoint her."

"Is that really the reason?"

"Frankly, no. The fact is I want to ask Muller a few more questions."

"Suppose he's not there?"

"Well, we shall just have to take a chance on that, shan't we?"

It was early afternoon on a dull, chilly day, with the London streets looking as though they were coming out in a cold sweat and the sky pressing down on the tops of the buildings like a dirty ceiling. Grant had called on Miss Donson after his interview with Mr Peking and had suggested that she might like to eat lunch with him.

"I believe you're setting up in the charity line," she said. "You think I'm starving now that I'm out of a job, so you're throwing me the odd meal to save my life."

"That's about it," Grant said. "I'd hate to lose you."

She hardly looked as though she were starving. In fact she looked very well-nourished and in the best of health. Being out of work and facing the prospect of having shortly to move out of her flat did not appear to be depressing her, either. She had not yet come to any decision regarding the suggestion Grant had made that she should move in with him, but he hoped she was giving it favourable consideration and would eventually fall in with the idea, because it seemed a pretty good one to him. Meanwhile, she seemed happy enough to give him the pleasure of her company, and he could not help reflecting that, though the job he was doing on Miss Rogerson's behalf might not be pulling in a great deal of cash for the Peking Agency, it certainly had its compensations as far as he was concerned.

She made no objection to the proposed call on Miss Harka after lunch.

"You haven't anything more important to do?" Grant asked.

"Like what? Looking for a job on a lousy winter's day? Anything would seem preferable to that."

"Even trailing around with me?"

She smiled and gave his arm a little squeeze. "Even that, Sam."

So he drove out to Clapham and rang the doorbell of the maisonette. And as luck would have it, both Angela and Kurt Muller were at home. From what Angela said Grant gathered that Muller had been out during the morning but had returned for lunch. She herself seemed delighted to welcome the visitors, but Muller did not look so pleased; in fact Grant would have made a guess that here was one very worried man, and he wondered just what it was that Muller had on his mind.

"I have been informed that you wished to have another look at me, Miss Harka," he said.

She glanced at Carol Donson. "You told him that?"

"Of course."

"You shouldn't have."

"Why not?"

"Because it's – well – embarrassing."

But she did not seem embarrassed. Faintly amused

perhaps, but certainly not embarrassed. She invited them to sit down and offered to make tea.

"No, don't bother," Miss Donson said. "At least, not for me. Do you want tea, Sam?"

"Not really. But thanks all the same, Miss Harka."

"Oh, please don't be so formal," she said. "If Carol is calling you Sam, I'm sure you can call me Angela."

"Thank you," Grant said. He turned to Muller, who was slumped in an armchair and apparently making a light meal of his knuckles. "And shall I call you Kurt?"

Muller looked annoyed. He answered in an angry, impatient tone of voice: "Let us finish with all this nonsense. We know you are not what you told us you were. You do not sell double-glazing; you are a private detective."

"Is that what you think?"

"It is what I know. Do you deny it?"

"No, I don't deny it."

"So why do you come here under false pretences?"

"Well," Grant said, "you know how it is: some people don't like having detectives around the house; it makes them feel uncomfortable. Especially when they have guilty consciences. Come to think of it, I'd say it makes you uncomfortable, Herr Muller."

"That is not so. Why should I be uncomfortable?"

"Why indeed! Surely you are the one who can answer that question."

"There is no question to be answered," Muller said. "I have told you I am not uncomfortable. I tell you again – I am not uncomfortable. Is that quite clear to you now, or must I repeat it once more?"

"Kurt, darling," Angela Harka said, "there's no need to get so heated about it."

Muller turned on her. "I am not heated, and I must ask you not to say that I am."

"Then why are you sweating?"

There were some beads of sweat on his forehead. He wiped them away with the back of his hand and fell again to gnawing at his knuckles.

Grant said: "I suppose I owe you an apology, Angela. I shouldn't have tried to pass myself off as a salesman."

"Oh, but isn't that all part of your profession?" she said. "I expect it comes almost as second nature to you to deceive people about yourself. It must be a fantastically interesting way of earning a living."

"It is a most underhand way of earning a living," Muller said.

Grant looked at him. "Is that your opinion?"

"You can be damn sure it is."

"Because of the little deception I indulged in?"

"Yes, because of that."

"And yet," Grant said musingly, "you yourself are also practising deception."

Muller sat up in his chair. "What do you mean by that?"

"I mean that you are not really here to gather material for a book, are you? You are not really a writer and it is doubtful whether your real name is Kurt Muller. So now that I've come clean, why don't you do the same? Tell us what your real name is and why you are in London. I am sure Angela would be as interested in that as any of us."

Muller seemed lost for an immediate answer; he sat biting his knuckles and glowering at his questioner but saying nothing. The girl was staring at him, wide-eyed.

"Kurt, what is the matter? It's not true, is it?"

He answered testily: "Of course it's not true. It is just Mr Grant's idea of a little bit of fun. He must have his joke. The famous English sense of humour, no?"

She looked at Grant. "Were you joking?"

"Of course," Grant said. "Just joking."

She said coldly: "I don't think I like that kind of joke."

"No? Then I apologise."

She seemed only half placated by the apology, and the atmosphere had suddenly become distinctly chilly. Carol Donson made an attempt to get things back to a more friendly footing, but it was no use; and after a few stiff and rather awkward exchanges she suggested to Grant that it was time to leave. He did not argue with that, and Angela showed no inclination to press them to stay. Muller sat in his chair saying nothing, just waiting for them to go.

"Now what," Miss Donson said, after they had left the house, "was that all about? Have you found any evidence that his name isn't Muller and that he's not a writer?"

"No evidence at all," Grant said. "I just threw out the suggestion to see how he'd take it."

"And were you satisfied with the result?"

"He reacted, didn't he? I think it touched a nerve."

"Oh, he certainly reacted. I've never seen him like that. The way he looked at you, I think he'd have been very happy to kill you."

"Now there's a funny thing; it's the very same thought that occurred to me."

"I wouldn't say it was funny," Miss Donson said. "Quite frankly, Sam, it frightens me."

*

Angela Harka looked at Muller. "What was he talking about, Kurt?"

Again Muller answered testily. "You heard him. You know as well as I do what he was talking about."

"But was there any truth in what he was saying?"

"Truth! Didn't you hear him say it was a joke?"

"I know he said that, but I don't think he was joking. I

think he really does believe you're not Kurt Muller."

"Really?" Muller said, faintly sneering. "And who do you suppose he thinks I am?"

"I don't know."

"Perhaps you, too, think I am not who I say I am. Do you want proof? Would you like me to show you my passport? Would that convince you?"

"You don't have to do that, Kurt."

"So you believe me?"

"Yes," she said, "I believe you. I just don't understand why you should have been so upset about it."

"I was not upset. The man annoys me, that is all. I should like to know why he is prying into my affairs."

"But he isn't. Why should you think he is? He's just a friend of Carol's."

"He is also a private detective, and men of that sort are not to be trusted."

"But does it matter whether he's to be trusted or not? You speak as though you had something to hide."

Muller stood up. "It is pointless to talk about this any more. I see that you are determined to believe the worst of me. I shall go for a walk."

"May I come with you?"

"No," he said firmly. "I would rather go alone."

She said nothing more; but when he had gone she went to the bedroom and began to look for the canvas holdall which he had carried with him on the previous two days. At first she was unable to find it, and she began to think it was not in the room; but when she took Muller's suitcase down from the top of the wardrobe so that she could look behind it, she could tell from its weight that it was not empty. She opened the suitcase and found the holdall stowed away inside. She saw that there was a slit in the canvas at one end, and when she opened the holdall she also found the knife.

She stared at the knife, puzzled and disturbed. On the point of the blade was a slight brown smear, which could have been paint. Muller had told her nothing about the knife. When she had asked him why he was taking the holdall with him he had said something about possibly buying some things while he was out; but there was nothing in the bag except this knife with the small stain on the blade. And why should he have bothered to hide the holdall? It could only be because he did not wish her to see what was inside it.

Doubts began to form in her mind. Suppose Grant had indeed not been joking. Suppose Kurt was not what he would have had her believe him to be. And if he were not, then what was he? And the knife! Why the knife? She shivered, as from a sudden chill. She closed the holdall, replaced it in the suitcase and fastened the lid. She put the suitcase back on the wardrobe where she had found it and left the bedroom with some most disturbing thoughts plaguing her mind.

*

Grant was back at his own flat by early evening. He had taken Carol Donson home after the rather abrasive call on Angela Harka and Kurt Muller, and Miss Donson had not seemed particularly eager for him to stick around. He got the impression that she was not terribly pleased with the way he had handled things at the maisonette; possibly she felt it might damage relations between her and Angela. Or maybe she was simply a bit tired of his company; which was not a thought that pleased him very much.

It was about seven o'clock when he had a visitor; a chunky man with a straggling moustache, glasses, a pasty complexion and a receding hairline. He introduced himself as Mr Jackson and asked if he might come in.

"I'd like a little talk with you, Mr Grant."

Grant had never seen him before, not that he could recollect; and he had a good memory for faces. Muller could have told him something about the man, because he had picked Muller up in Ipswich in a yellow Allegro and later had driven him up to London. Muller could have told him that the man had been calling himself Carl at that time; but Muller was not there to tell him anything, and might not have been willing to do so if he had been.

Grant was not exactly eager to have a talk with Mr Jackson, but he let him into the flat and offered him a chair.

"So you know my name."

"Yes," Jackson said. "You were recommended to me."

"Is that so? By whom and in what connection?"

Jackson smiled. "Let us not bother with the name. You are a private inquiry agent, Mr Grant."

"That's right."

"I hear you are good."

"I'm glad somebody thinks so."

"I would like to employ you."

Grant shook his head. "You can't do that. I work for the Peking Inquiry Agency. You have to go to the office; I don't take on jobs personally."

"That is a pity," Jackson said; but he did not seem devastated by the information. He was taking a good look at the room, as if making a mental note of the contents. "Nice little place you have here."

"It's not nice," Grant said, "but it's somewhere to live. Better than sleeping on a park bench."

"Bedroom through there?" Mr Jackson pointed a stubby finger.

"Yes, the bedroom's through there. And there's a kitchenette over there. But I don't think you came here to discuss the accommodation."

"That's true. I thought you might be able to help me."

"In what way?"

"To find a man."

"I'm sorry," Grant said. "As I told you, you'll have to go to the office." He was not at all sure he would have wanted to work for Jackson anyway; he was not sure he liked the look of the man. And with his accent, what was he doing with a name like that?

"Well," Jackson said, "if that's the way it is –" He got up from the chair. "I suppose I can ask them to put you on the job?"

"You can ask, but it will depend on how the work is lined up whether or not you'll get me."

Jackson grinned at him, revealing a gap in his teeth. "Oh, I think I'll get you, Mr Grant. I think I'll get you."

After he had gone Grant made himself a cup of strong coffee and gave some thought to his would-be client. He had a feeling that there was something phoney about Jackson. There was that accent of his for a start: he spoke English well enough, but certainly not as a native of the United Kingdom. Was his name really Jackson? And if not, what was his game? And who was the mysterious person who had given the recommendation? There was altogether too much mystery hanging around Mr Jackson for Grant's liking, too many questions without answers.

Well, there was no point in bothering himself about the matter; he would just have to wait until the morning. No doubt Jackson would divulge a bit more information when he called in at the offices of the Peking Inquiry Agency.

Always supposing he did call in.

14

AWAY WE GO

The car was a blue Renault. Puskis was driving; Stanev was sitting beside him and Tomic was in the back. It was getting on for one o'clock in the morning and it was freezing hard. There had been a light fall of snow earlier, but it had stopped now and the sky had cleared, allowing the moon to show itself.

Puskis drove carefully. He and the others were armed, and if they had been involved in an accident and the police had found the guns an awkward situation might have arisen, since the weapons were not licensed. Besides, there was no need to drive fast; they were not pushed for time; the rest of the night lay ahead of them and that meant six or seven more hours before daylight.

It was a few minutes past one when they reached the Clapham area, and Stanev was giving Puskis directions. Puskis was driving quite slowly now, and when they came to the right road Stanev told him to pull in to the kerb about thirty yards short of the maisonette. Puskis stopped the car and switched off the ignition and the lights.

"Now," Stanev said, "we all know what to do. You, Emil, will remain in the car, and as soon as you see us returning you will start the engine. Milan and I will go to the door and ring the bell. If Muller opens it we will take him at once. If it is the girl who comes we will go straight in, silence her and then take Muller. That is understood?"

It was understood; there had really been no need to repeat the plan of action; it was all very simple and straightforward, and they had already discussed it thoroughly. None of them had been able to see any reason why it should go wrong.

Stanev took a snub-nosed revolver from his pocket and twirled the cylinder to check that it was fully loaded. Tomic had an old Mauser automatic, a big, ugly gun with the magazine in front of the trigger guard and a grip like the sawn-off end of a broomstick; it had a wooden holster which could be fitted to the gun to serve as a stock if you wanted to take really careful aim.

The road was quiet and deserted. Everybody in the neighbourhood seemed to have gone to bed.

"Right, then," Stanev said. "Let us go."

He and Tomic got out of the car and began to walk towards the maisonette along the snow-covered pavement. They had taken no more than a few steps when a yellow car came up from behind, passed them and drew to a halt by the kerb a short distance further on. Stanev put a hand on Tomic's arm and they both stopped walking.

"What now?" Tomic asked.

"Wait," Stanev said.

There was only one man in the yellow car. He got out and walked straight up to the door of the maisonette without a glance to left or right. The door had apparently been left unlocked, for he simply turned the knob, pushed it open and disappeared inside.

"So," Stanev said, "Muller has another visitor."

"That was not Muller?"

"No, it was not at all like him. And obviously this man was expected; the door had been left unlocked."

"It is very late for a visitor to arrive."

"Yes. And it is also awkward, from our point of view."

"So what do we do now?"

"I think," Stanev said, "that we go back to our car and wait. Let us hope the visitor does not stay too long."

They returned to the blue Renault and got in.

"So we have a complication," Puskis said. "Perhaps it is best now to call it off for tonight."

"Not yet," Stanev said.

Puskis shrugged and said no more. They settled down to wait as the air in the car became gradually colder. Tomic hummed a tune very softly, and Puskis took out a handkerchief and blew his nose.

Fifteen minutes later the door of the maisonette opened and two men came out and walked to the car parked outside. One of the men was carrying a suitcase and a small holdall, both of which he put into the boot.

"That is Muller," Stanev said.

"With luggage," Tomic said. "What in hell is going on?"

"It looks as if he's moving out."

"So we could lose him."

"We must not lose him."

"Then what do we do?"

"Follow the yellow car," Stanev said. "Start the engine, Emil."

*

Angela Harka woke suddenly to the realisation that someone was moving in the darkness of the bedroom. She reached out a hand, groped for the bedside light and switched it on, revealing Muller standing by the wardrobe and in the act of taking down the suitcase which only a few hours earlier she herself had put back in its place.

Muller was fully dressed, and it took her a few seconds to

remember that he had not retired to bed when she had. He had returned quite late from his walk, but had refused to say where he had been and had seemed to be in no better temper than when he had left the house. He had declined to eat any supper, saying brusquely that he was not hungry, but he had drunk two or three glasses of whisky, which had not noticeably improved his temper.

Once or twice she had thought of questioning him about the knife in the holdall, but he had been so morose that she had decided it was not a propitious moment and that she had better leave it for another day. She had never seen him so moody, and when she had suggested that it was time for bed he had told her not to wait for him because he was going to do some writing and he could only do it if he were left to himself. So with some misgiving, she had left him on his own and had gone to bed.

Muller, surprised by the sudden switching on of the light, paused with his hands still raised to grasp the suitcase on top of the wardrobe and looked at the girl in the bed. But he said nothing.

"What are you doing?" she said.

He took the suitcase down and placed it on the floor. "I should have thought you could see what I am doing," he said, with a faint sneer.

She glanced at the bedside clock. "Do you know how late it is? What can you want with your suitcase at this time of night?"

"Yes," he said, "I do know how late it is. But there is something in the suitcase that I have need of."

"You mean the knife," she said.

She had spoken without thinking; it was the first thing that had flashed into her mind, and the words had slipped from her tongue before she could hold them back. She regretted the impetuosity almost immediately and wished she had remained silent.

"Ah!" Muller said, very softly. "So you know what is inside the case. You have been prying into my belongings, meddling with things that do not concern you. Was that entirely wise, do you think?"

She detected a hint of menace in his voice, and it frightened her. From the moment when she had discovered the knife she had begun to see this man in a far more sinister light. Until then she had believed him, trusted him; now the clouds of infatuation were dispersing and she was becoming aware of a darker side of his character; awakening to the realisation that she knew so little about him and that what she did not know could be terrifying indeed.

"Surely," she said, and despite all her efforts to control it her voice trembled slightly, "anything that concerns you concerns me as well. Surely I have some right to know what you are doing."

Muller shook his head. "Oh, no. You overrate your importance, my dear. You should not imagine that because I have been living with you, sleeping with you, making love to you, this gives you the right to know anything more regarding me than I choose to tell you."

"You have been lying to me," she said.

"Naturally. What would you expect?"

She stared at him, as though seeing him for the first time. "I don't know you. I have never known you, have I?"

"No, you have never known me."

"Who are you? What are you?"

He gave a hard laugh. "Do you really expect me to tell you that?" He opened the suitcase, removed the holdall, took out the knife and showed it to her. "Do you know what this is on the blade? It is blood – a man's blood."

She shuddered and drew away from him. "You killed a man?"

"Unfortunately, no. He escaped."

"But you tried to kill him?"

He shrugged. "You ask so many questions. You should never have started asking questions; you should have remained blind; it was safer that way. Now you have become a problem. Shortly I must leave the house; but what am I to do with you? Knowing what you do, little as it is, you have become a danger to me. When I am gone you may immediately start doing things that could be a danger to me. I cannot afford to let that happen." He looked at the knife in his hand. "You see the way it is?"

She stared at the knife, at the brown stain which she now knew was the dried blood of a man. "You wouldn't kill me!"

"What choice do I have? I must think of my own safety."

"I will say nothing. Go away. Leave me. I promise not to do anything to harm you."

"A woman will promise anything to save her own life. But afterwards, when the danger is past, what then?"

"I swear to you —"

"No, it is not enough." He reached out suddenly and gripped her right arm with his left hand. She struggled to free herself, but his grasp was too strong. She managed to get her legs out of the bed on the opposite side, and she was lying across it, still trying to free herself, when she heard the sound of the front door opening and closing and of someone moving around in the entrance hall. She had no idea who it could be or how the intruder could have got into the house, but she gave a cry for help; anyone would surely come to her aid in such a situation.

"Stop that!" Muller said. He hauled her further across the bed and put the knife to her neck. "Keep quiet or I will cut your throat."

She could feel the cold edge of the blade touching her skin, and it silenced her. She lay still, no longer struggling, and she heard the intruder coming up the stairs. From where she was lying she had a view of the door; and she saw it open and a man come into the room.

"You have some trouble?" the man said; and he was not speaking to her but to Muller.

He was someone she had never seen before, and she still could not understand how it was that the front door had been unlocked or why he should have walked into the house without even ringing the bell.

Then Muller said: "A little trouble, yes. She found the knife."

"That is a pity," the man said; and he looked at Angela Harka, stroking his chin thoughtfully with his left hand. "Now we shall have to do something about it."

She saw that he had a pale round face and a moustache and glasses. If Grant had been there he would have recognised him as Mr Jackson, but Muller knew him only by the name of Carl. Miss Harka knew him by neither name, but she knew now that she could expect no help from him.

Muller took the knife away from her neck and released her arm. "Get up," he said.

She got off the bed on the opposite side from the two men and stood up. Carl looked her up and down. She was wearing only a brief nightdress, so filmy that it concealed very little of her body.

"Very nice," Carl said. "Very nice indeed." He turned to Muller. "A pity she has to be killed."

Muller looked troubled; he was thinking of the woman in Bonn whom he had been ordered to kill, and what a messy business it had been. He still had bad dreams about that.

"Perhaps it will not be necessary to do that," he said. "It will surely be enough if we tie her up and leave her. Whatever happens, I cannot come back here now "

"And you think she will not talk?"

"What does it matter if she does talk? She knows nothing."

"She knows you."

"She will never see me again."

"I still say it is better to silence her."

"No; I cannot agree to it."

Carl gave a mocking grin. "You are too soft, my friend. Because she is young and lovely, and because you have slept with her, you cannot bring yourself to stick a knife into her sweet body. Well, I am a generous man; I will do it for you. Or better, I will smother her with a pillow; it is a cleaner way."

"No," Muller said again. "We will tie her up."

Carl made a gesture of resignation. "You are a fool; but if that is what you wish —"

Angela had been watching them, knowing that her life was trembling in the balance, praying that Muller would stand firm and not allow himself to be persuaded by the other man. She felt almost giddy with relief when Muller had his way, and she made no resistance when he ordered her to lie on the bed while he tied her arms and legs with the belts from two of her own dresses. Then he gagged her with a handkerchief and a stocking. The other man took no hand in the operation but stood looking on with a sardonic grin twisting his mouth.

When Muller had completed the trussing of the girl he began to throw his clothes and other gear hastily into the suitcase and the holdall. She watched him from the bed. It had all started with a mugging in a narrow street, and it was ending like this. Tears blurred her vision, and it was through a veil of tears that she saw him go out of the room at the back of the other man.

He had not spoken a word of goodbye and had not thrown as much as a backward glance at the girl he had made use of and so cruelly deceived. She was fortunate to have escaped with her life; it was only his weakness that had saved her. She knew it, but it made the mental hurt he had caused her no less difficult to bear.

*

Grant awoke from a pleasant dream of the lovely Carol Donson to something far less pleasant – something cold and sharp pricking him under the chin. The door of the bedroom was open and there was some light coming in from the living-room; enough to reveal the shadowy figure of a man bending over him.

"Quiet now," the man said. "Don't do anything rash."

He recognised the voice as that of Kurt Muller; and then someone switched the bedroom light on and another man came into his line of sight, a visitor who had called on him some hours previously and had given his name as Jackson. He could not see what it was that Muller was using to prick the soft flesh below his chin, but he had no difficulty in guessing that it was a knife. And as if to make even more certain that he did nothing rash, Mr Jackson produced a pistol that looked remarkably like a Luger. He was not pointing it at Grant; he was just holding it in his right hand and letting it dangle at his side.

Muller took the knife away from Grant's chin and stepped back a pace. "Get dressed," he said.

"Why?" Grant asked.

"You're coming with us."

"I'd much rather not, if you don't mind."

"But we do mind," Jackson said. "Don't argue. Do as he says."

Grant looked at the Luger in Jackson's hand and the knife in Muller's. "You have some pretty strong arguments," he said. "So I won't argue." He got off the bed and began to dress. "Just as a matter of interest, how did you get in?"

Jackson gave a soft chuckle. "It was not difficult. You should do something about the locks, Mr Grant."

"I've been thinking about that. Maybe I'll get round to it some day."

"Some day could be too late."

"I see what you mean. I take it that your earlier call was just a piece of reconnaissance? This isn't a way of persuading me to take that job you were talking about?"

"No."

"I was afraid not."

He finished dressing and made a move towards the wardrobe.

"Stop!" Muller said. "What are you doing?"

Grant stopped. "I was just going to get something warm to put on. I imagine it's still cold outside."

"I'll get it," Muller said. He opened the wardrobe. "What do you want?"

"The anorak."

Muller took out the blue quilted anorak and felt the pockets before handing it to Grant.

"No weapons," Grant said. "I'm a peaceful man."

"You are also an inquisitive man. Too inquisitive for your own good."

"Oh, is that what this is all about? The questions I asked you. You really must have a guilty conscience."

"Never mind my conscience." Muller sounded angry. "Who are you working for?"

Grant slipped the anorak on. "Would you believe an elderly maiden lady living in a quiet country village?"

"Now he is being funny," Jackson said. "Why waste time? Let's go."

"Are we going far?" Grant asked.

"Far enough."

"Then I think I'd better go to the bathroom first."

"All right, but get on with it."

"That's what I intend to do."

Muller went with him; they were taking no chances. And even if they had let him go alone, what could he have done? A monkey might have escaped by the window, but he was no monkey; and there was no weapon in the bathroom more lethal than a toothbrush or a toilet-roll. He zipped up and preceded Muller into the living-room, where Jackson was waiting.

"Are you ready now?" Jackson asked.

"I'm ready," Grant said. "I'd still rather not go with you, but if you insist —"

"We do insist."

They switched off all the lights and closed the door of the flat before descending the stairs. Muller stayed close to Grant with the knife in his hand and warned him not to make any noise.

"I could slip this into you very easily," he whispered.

"I think you'd rather enjoy that," Grant said; and he was whispering too, because Muller might consider he was making a noise if he raised his voice; and that length of sharp, pointed steel was not something he wished to feel sliding into his flesh.

There was snow on the pavement and on the roofs of the houses, making it all look very wintry; and the air had a frosty bite in it. Grant could see a yellow Allegro standing by the kerb, and further up the road a blue Renault which as far as he could make out had nobody in it. He would have been very glad to see a patrolling police car, but there was not one in sight, and no copper on the beat either.

Jackson opened the rear door of the Allegro and told Grant to get in; he had the Luger in his hand and was probably quite prepared to use it, so Grant decided to obey the order. Muller followed him and closed the door; he was still keeping the knife handy. Jackson got into the driver's seat and started the car.

"So away we go," Grant said.

"Yes," Muller said, "away we go."

15

A DEAD MAN

Grant had been wrong in supposing the blue Renault to be empty. There were in fact three men in it, but they were keeping their heads down in case either Muller or the driver of the other car happened to glance in their direction; it might have struck them as odd that three men should have been sitting in a stationary vehicle in a quiet residential road at that hour of a cold December morning.

The three men had seen Muller and his companion go into the house, and they had seen a light come on in one of the second-floor windows.

"Now what are the swine doing?" Tomic said.

"Calling on a friend?" Puskis suggested.

"A damn strange time of night to call on a friend. An enemy, maybe, but not a friend."

"Let us wait and see what happens," Stanev said.

A little later they saw the light go out in the upper window; then Muller and the driver came out with another man, all three bunched closely together. From where they were watching it was impossible to see any weapons, but they doubted whether the third man had come willingly.

"They got him out of bed," Tomic said. "Nobody gets out of bed in the middle of the night without persuasion. I wonder what they used to persuade him."

They heard the faint sound of the doors of the other car as they were pulled shut and saw the lights come on.

"Do I still follow them?" Puskis asked.

"You still follow them," Stanev said.

It was not difficult to keep the yellow car in sight; it was not speeding and it showed up clearly under the street-lamps. At one point a small pick-up truck squeezed in between the two cars, but Puskis was not worried; he could still see the yellow Allegro and it was well not to be too close on its tail in case the driver became suspicious.

They came to the Camden Road, crossed the Holloway Road and kept travelling in a north-easterly direction until they reached Woodford and then Romford and headed towards Basildon.

"Where the devil are they going?" Tomic said.

"Southend perhaps," Stanev suggested.

But he was wrong; about a mile farther on the Allegro turned off on to a minor road and was soon making its way along narrow winding lanes where it was difficult for Puskis to keep it in sight without getting dangerously close.

"Don't lose them," Stanev said. "For God's sake don't lose them now."

"I'm not going to lose them," Puskis said; but five minutes later he had to confess that he had. There was half a mile of straight road ahead, bright moonlight, and no sign of any other car. The Allegro had simply vanished.

"They can't have got that far ahead," Stanev said. "What happened to them?"

Puskis stopped the car. "It was not my fault. These roads—"

Tomic began to swear.

*

Jackson had been aware of the other car on his tail for some time. He spoke about it to Muller.

"We are being followed."

"Are you sure?" Muller said.

"I am sure."

"But who would be following us?"

"The police," Grant suggested.

But he did not believe it. His personal opinion was that Jackson was imagining things. Even if the car behind them had been there for some time, it was no more than a coincidence; it just happened to be going in the same direction. Nevertheless, when they turned off the major road and the other car still hung on it did begin to look like something more than mere chance. At that time of night traffic on the lanes and byways they were now following was practically non-existent, and the car on their tail became more conspicuous. He began to take more interest in it then, because, police or no police, if someone was following them it could have a profound effect on his fortunes.

From the start of the journey he had been under no illusions as to what was happening: the ride for which he was being taken was intended to be a return trip for two and a one-way journey for one. And he was the one, the odd man out. Mr Peking had told him to lean on Muller in the hope of scaring him off. Well, he had leaned a bit; not very heavily, but enough; Muller had taken fright without a doubt, but the result of his fright had not been quite what Peking had expected. Instead of being scared off, Muller had decided to remove the one who was doing the leaning, and he had called in a bit of help in the shape of this character who said his name was Jackson. So much for Peking's brilliant schemes. Another time he would work things out his own way and let Peking just deal with the clients – if there ever was another time.

During the course of the journey he had flogged his brain in an effort to figure out a way of escape. If he could take

Muller by surprise, wrest the knife from him, put him out of
action and then threaten Jackson with the knife ...

But Jackson was armed, and as soon as anything started
happening in the back he would stop the car and pull out
the gun. So it would be essential to deal with Muller very
quickly. The trouble was that Muller was so very much on
the alert. Grant made one or two tentative moves just to test
him, and always Muller was quick to bring the knife into
play; so that all Grant got for his pains was a slight cut on
the left wrist – as a warning. Finally he decided to wait until
the end of the journey and look for his chance then.

When Jackson spoke about the following car it was
apparent that Muller was worried; he kept glancing
through the rear window to see if it was still there. He
suggested to Jackson that he should push up the speed and
try to shake it off.

"These roads are no good for speeding," Jackson said.
"And that other car is probably as fast as this – if not faster.
I will slow and see if it passes."

He did so, but the other car stayed behind.

"That proves it," Muller said. "They are tailing us."

Jackson gave a laugh. "Don't let it bother you. I will lose
them very soon."

His opportunity came soon after that. There was a high
wall on their right, probably enclosing a small estate, and
the road bent sharply in that direction. The following car
had fallen back slightly and was a hundred yards or so
behind. Jackson took the Allegro fast round the bend and
out of sight of the other car. There was a hedge on the left
and a gap suddenly appeared in it. Without hesitation
Jackson braked hard and swung the Allegro off the road
and into the opening. The moment they were through the
gap he switched the lights off, and for a short distance they
went forward with only the light of the moon, bumping and
swaying over the rough, snow-covered ground, before he

pulled the car to a halt. A moment later they heard the
other car come round the bend and saw the lights sweep
past and disappear.

"So much for them," Jackson said. And then: "I think
this could be a very suitable place for what we have to do,
don't you?"

In the moonlight it was possible to see that they were on
a kind of farm track, with a hedge on the right and a
barbed-wire fence on the left, beyond which the ground
stretched, flat and white under the snow, to a dark belt of
trees. Jackson got the car moving again, but did not switch
on the lights. Grant had a hand on the catch of the door at
his side and was waiting for the best opportunity to fling it
open and make his bid to escape. The track curved to the
right and suddenly a building came into view, discernible
only as a dark shape against the sky.

"Stop!" Muller said sharply. "There's a house."

The car had been travelling only very slowly, grinding
along in low gear, and as Muller spoke Grant swung his left
fist, striking him with a backhanded blow on the side of the
face. Muller gave a cry, and at the same instant Grant
pushed the door open and jumped out.

The car had not quite come to a stop, and as his feet
touched the ground he stumbled and fell forward on to his
hands and knees. He was up in a moment, however, and
began sprinting towards the building some fifty yards
ahead. He reckoned that Jackson had two alternatives: he
could either get the car going again and try to catch him
before he made it to the building or he could bring it to a
complete halt and take a shot with the Luger. In the event
he chose the latter course, but he must have taken a few
seconds to make up his mind, and when the first shot came
Grant was almost at the building.

He had no set plan in his mind, but he thought it likely
that the place was a farmhouse or possibly a farm-worker's

cottage, though it seemed rather large for that, and he had some vague hope of rousing the occupants and getting help or refuge. Perhaps somebody would have a shotgun, and anyway Jackson and Muller might hesitate to carry out their design on the very doorstep of an inhabited dwelling.

A couple of seconds later he realised that he could put any idea of obtaining assistance completely out of his mind, for the building turned out to be nothing better than a dilapidated barn, with some sheds and a stockyard adjoining it. There were no animals in the stockyard; possibly it had not been used for years; and there were certainly no human beings anywhere near except himself and Jackson and Muller.

Jackson had fired only two shots, and then had apparently decided that it was a waste of time and ammunition at that range. Now Grant could hear the two men running down the track in pursuit, having left the car where it was.

There were two high wooden doors on the barn, falling to pieces and hanging askew. Grant had an impulse to run inside and try to hide; it was instinctive, like a hunted animal taking refuge in a hole. But it would have been a foolish thing to do; it would have been to put himself in a trap, and he resisted the impulse.

The ground in front of the barn was uneven, rutted mud frozen hard and sprinkled with snow. Grant twisted an ankle as he ran towards the fence of the stockyard on the right of the barn and he could feel the pain of it as he climbed over the fence and dropped on the other side on to a thick mattress of old rotting straw.

He heard Jackson and Muller reach the barn, but they seemed to have lost sight of him for a moment, and he ploughed his way through the straw and got to the fence on the other side of the yard. He began to climb the fence, and when he had reached the top rail he looked back and could

see the piece of ground in front of the barn, half in shadow
and half glimmering whitely in the moonlight. He had
expected to see the two men, but they seemed to have
vanished. Then he caught sight of them standing in the
doorway of the barn and peering into the gloom inside. It
was evident that they thought he might have gone in there,
as he had indeed had an inclination to do; and then he
heard Muller shouting.

"Grant! Come out! Or must we come in and get you?"

Grant decided to get away while their attention was
elsewhere, and he was about to climb down on the far side
of the stockyard and make off in that direction when he
caught sight of what appeared like a broad black line drawn
across the white page of the snow. He knew at once what it
was; it was a dyke or drainage ditch. It looked too wide to
jump, even without the handicap of a twisted ankle, and
was probably too deep to wade. He glanced to the right and
to the left, but in each direction there was a flat expanse of
field or pasture with its pale covering of snow. Against such
a background a running man would show up clearly in the
moonlight, and he had no wish to be hunted down like an
animal and shot in the open. Besides, how could he run
with that damned ankle giving way under him?

The fence joined up with an open-fronted shed that had
once provided shelter for the bullocks that had been
fattened there, and he saw that by standing on the top rail
he could reach up to the sloping pantiled roof and perhaps
climb on to it. Then, if he lay flat, he would be invisible
from the yard and his two pursuers might assume that he
had managed to slip away while they had been looking into
the barn. He had no sooner thought of this plan than he
began to put it into operation. One or two of the tiles were
missing at the edge of the roof, and he was able to get a grip
on the exposed slats, haul himself up and get one knee over
the edge. With a heave he brought the other leg up.

He was now stretched out on the upper edge of the roof, and he started to wriggle his body into a position where he would be lying along the slope of the tiles, a foot or two from the top. Unfortunately, the roof was in bad repair; some of the timbers were worm-eaten and rotten, while many of the tiles were chipped or flaking. Under his weight a slat cracked loudly and a tile broke where his left knee was resting, the pieces falling through to the floor of the shed below. He immediately shifted his position further to the right, fearful of sliding down the roof, which had been made slippery by snow, and hoping that the noise had not been heard by the two men in the barn. But it was too much to hope; he heard them coming, and then heard Jackson's voice only a few feet away.

"It must have been him. He must be somewhere around."

Then it was Muller's voice. "Perhaps he is in the shed."

He heard someone below him then, apparently searching the shed; and then Jackson's voice again, slightly muffled.

"No, he's not here. It is dark, but I am sure he is not in here."

It was Muller who guessed the truth. "So perhaps he is on the roof." He raised his voice. "Are you up there, Grant? Do you think you can escape us that way?"

Grant said nothing; he lay very still, feeling the cold dampness penetrating his trousers where the snow had melted under the warmth of his body. He had his left cheek pressed against the tiles, and that was cold too.

"I feel sure he is up there," Muller said. He was speaking to Jackson, who appeared to be still inside the shed. "He is keeping quiet to try to fool us. But he is up there sure enough."

"There is a way of finding out," Jackson said, with a laugh.

Grant wondered what Jackson found so damned

amusing; but he did not have long to wait before finding out. He heard the crack of the Luger, and one of the tiles a foot or two away on his right disintegrated as if it had suddenly exploded. Something hit him on the chin, and he guessed that it was a splinter of baked clay.

He heard Jackson's mocking voice. "Are you all right, Mr Grant? Do you think you will be making your report to Mr Peking? I have a lot of bullets left."

As if to prove it, he fired again, and another tile exploded a little further down the roof. Grant lay still, but his skin crawled; he knew that sooner or later a bullet was going to come up through the roof just where he was lying, unless Jackson gave up; and he did not think that was likely. Another tile flew into fragments; it was close to his right leg and he felt some of the pieces hit him on the ankle. He thought of sliding off the roof and taking a chance on what might lie below the lower edge; but he might break a leg, and where would that get him? He did not move.

The pistol cracked again, and this time it was a tile on the other side that disintegrated. Jackson had bracketed him; he seemed to have a pretty shrewd idea of where his target was, so perhaps he had found the tile that had fallen through to the floor and had drawn his conclusions from that. How many more shots before he got the correct line and smashed a hole in his victim's pelvis or stomach or chest? Grant found himself shivering uncontrollably, and it seemed to him that the shivering must communicate itself to the entire shed, shaking the tiles and making the timbers creak.

"Soon now, Mr Grant," Jackson said, taunting him. And Grant could tell that the man was just below the place where he was lying.

So perhaps he knew; perhaps he was levelling the pistol for that final shot, the one that would tear the flesh apart. Grant had an urge to cry out, to beg Jackson not to fire; but he said nothing, made no cry, no appeal, but simply lay on the cold tiles – waiting for the shot.

But it did not come. Instead, there was a totally unexpected interruption. A man shouted:

"Muller! Kurt Muller!"

The voice seemed to be coming from the direction of the fence on the barn side of the stockyard. Grant heard a movement in the shed, as though Jackson had walked out of it to see who was shouting; and then he heard Muller's voice, and could tell that Muller was afraid.

"Who is that?"

"Never mind who this is," the voice from the fence said. "You are a dead man, Muller, a dead man."

Grant could not remain still any longer; he had to see what was happening. He pulled himself up to the top edge of the roof and peered over it. He had a glimpse of three men standing by the fence; and then one of them switched on a powerful hand-lamp, and Muller and Jackson were caught in the beam. He heard Jackson give a curse; and he brought the Luger up and fired at the men by the fence.

It was as though he had touched the triggers of their guns, and suddenly they were all firing. One of them sounded to Grant like a submachine-gun; he did not know until later that it was Tomic's Mauser and that Tomic was using the wooden holster as a stock.

The man who had shouted had been telling the truth: Muller was indeed a dead man. He was lying on the old rotten straw and the snow, and Jackson was lying beside him, dead too; full of bullets and still and bloody and dead.

"Christ." Grant muttered. "Christ, what a bloody shambles!"

He rested his forehead on the cold snow and tried to control the shivering that was uncontrollable.

16

VERY SATISFACTORY

They took him home in the blue Renault. They told him
they had been following the yellow car because they had
urgent business with one of the men in it. They had lost it,
but they had come back and found the wheel-marks in the
snow where it had turned off the road. They had switched
off their lights and followed the track until they had come to
the other car. They had heard the sound of shooting and
they had come quickly then, and that was all.

They did not tell him who they were or why they had
killed the men. The one who was sitting beside the driver
said: "It is best you do not know."

Grant went along with that. He had no wish to know
their names, no wish to know anything about them. The
man with the Mauser looked a tough baby, and Grant was
glad they had no quarrel with him.

It was getting on for six o'clock in the morning when they
put him down at his place in Camden Town. They knew
where he lived because they had seen him abducted, but
they did not ask him his name and he did not tell them. It
was best that way too.

When they had gone he walked to the lock-up garage
where he kept his car, and got it out and drove to the
maisonette in Clapham. His twisted ankle was swollen and

painful, but he was worried about Angela Harka. Nobody came when he rang the bell, but he found the door unlocked, and he went in and looked in the rooms on the ground floor; and then he climbed the stairs and went into the bedroom and switched on the light. The girl was lying on the bed where Muller had left her, bound and gagged.

She stared up at him as if he had been a man risen from the dead, and even when he had removed the gag she said nothing, just waited for him to release her wrists and ankles.

"You are all right?" he asked.

She did not answer the question. She was still lying on the bed, still staring up at him as though even yet finding it hard to believe he was really there.

"You!" she whispered at last. "So they didn't –"

He guessed what she would have said. "No, they didn't kill me. But they tried. It was a damned close thing."

"There's blood on your face, and on your hand."

"It's nothing."

She was sitting up now, shivering, chafing her wrists. She seemed to have difficulty in forming the next question, but she got it out at last, though her voice was so low it was scarcely audible.

"And Kurt?"

"He will not be coming back," Grant said.

She asked no more; she looked into his eyes, and perhaps she guessed what he had not said. And suddenly she was clinging to him, weeping and trembling, her face pressed against his chest. He put his arms round her and held her for a time. Then he said:

"I think you had better get dressed now. I'll wait downstairs."

When she came down she had regained control of herself. She was pale and red-eyed, but she looked composed.

"I've been a fool," she said. "I realise that now. I'm not

going to ask you what it was all about —"

"That's just as well," Grant said, "because I'm pretty much in the dark myself. I just know it must have been something damned nasty. You're well out of it. Now get your coat and we'll be going."

"Going where?"

"To Carol's place. I think you need another shoulder to cry on."

She did not argue. She got her coat and they went out to the car. They exchanged hardly a word on the journey through a London that was only just waking to another day, and not apparently liking it much.

Miss Donson came to the door in a dressing-gown, and she was sensible enough not to waste time in asking a lot of questions on the doorstep; she just told them to come in. She glanced at Grant's face and hand.

"You've been in trouble," she said.

"A little."

"You look terrible and you need a shave."

"I'll settle for a cup of strong, hot coffee."

"I think we could all use some of that," she said, and she went to make it.

He did not stay long after drinking the coffee. He went back to his own flat and made some more of the same, and had a bath and went to bed. He felt that he had some sleep owing to him.

*

Mr Peking was looking very smug, Grant thought, with a touch of resentment; like a very large fat cat that had been at the cream.

"All things considered," Mr Peking said, "I think we have cause to be reasonably well pleased. Everything seems to have turned out very satisfactorily, very satisfactorily indeed."

After much thought Grant had decided not to give Peking all the gory details of the affair; the less said about that, the better. Mr Peking might have felt it his duty to call in the police, and that would only have led to undesirable complications. So he had merely told his employer that he had carried out his instructions: he had leaned on Muller and it had had the desired effect.

The bodies of Jackson and Muller would be found, of course; but there might be some difficulty in identifying them because the other three men had emptied their pockets and taken away everything that might have revealed who they were. It was doubtful whether the true identity of Jackson would be discovered even from the abandoned car, and if Muller was ever identified it would certainly not be under that name.

"Are you going to tell Miss Rogerson?" Grant asked. "Or do you want me to do that?"

"You, I think, Grant. It was your case and we can spare you for a little longer. Take another trip down into the country and reassure her. I am sure it will greatly relieve her mind to hear that things have turned out so well."

"Oh, I'm sure it will," Grant said.

Peking seemed to detect a certain lack of enthusiasm. "What's the matter with you? You don't look altogether pleased. A trifle glum, in fact."

Grant felt that he had some reason to feel a trifle glum. He was thinking of a flat which would not after all be having the charming Miss Donson to liven it up. Because the fact was, now that Muller had gone away and would not be coming back, Miss Harka had decided to return to Miss Donson's flat; and Miss Donson had found another job and had had second thoughts about moving in with a private eye.

"I'm very fond of you, Sam," she said, "but I don't think it would have worked. Sorry."

Grant was sorry too; he was probably a lot more sorry than she was, but there was nothing he could do about it; perhaps he had already done too much, in getting rid of Muller and leaving Miss Harka free to return to the old abode.

"What is the trouble, Grant?" Peking asked.

"The trouble," Grant said, "is that my private life is not in such a happy state as I had hoped it might be. I think that from my point of view it would have been a hell of a lot better if I'd never leaned on Muller at all, and that's a fact."

Mr Peking stared at him. "You know, Grant," he said, "there are times when I simply don't understand you, by Jupiter, I don't."